Boyd Rode Alone

Alvin Boyd was a killer, not a bad man, but when he tried to escape his past, he found he stood alone. After Alvin's death, his brother, Asa, rode into town looking to avenge him. What he found was a white-hot range war. Quickly finding a job as the town's deputy, Asa found it to be a tough job in this hard-fighting trail town and Asa found new enemies that included a murderous land baron and a deadly gunfighter. Caught in the dangerous crossfire between ranchers and moneymen, maddened by the murders of his brother and others, Asa Boyd's reward would be simple – the love of a beautiful woman.

He had nothing to lose but his life!

Boyd Rode Alone

Matt Cole

A Black Horse Western

ROBERT HALE

© Matt Cole 2018
First published in Great Britain 2018

ISBN 978-0-7198-2858-4

The Crowood Press
The Stable Block
Crowood Lane
Ramsbury
Marlborough
Wiltshire SN8 2HR

www.bhwesterns.com

Robert Hale is an imprint
of The Crowood Press

Typeset by
Derek Doyle & Associates, Shaw Heath
Printed and bound in Great Britain by
4Bind Ltd, Stevenage, SG1 2XT

PROLOGUE

Alvin Boyd was a killer. He confirmed it now as he backed slowly out of the Alcove Springs Bank with a smoking Colt in one hand and a gunnysack full of money in the other. The teller had made a move for the pistol underneath the money counter. Alvin Boyd's bullet had caught the unfortunate man between the eyes.

The cashier, his actions sluggish from utter fear, made a break for the side door and was shot in the back.

'You'll be next,' he told the young lady stenographer, 'if you say one word.'

The snowstorm outside stifled the sound of the shots. There was no one out in the little storm-swept cow town to hinder Alvin Boyd's departure. He mounted the horse that stood huddled in the snow. In five minutes, he was lost in the snowstorm, made thicker by the shadows of dusk. He left no revealing sign. Because the country between the Little Blue River and the border of Nebraska was as familiar as a child's back yard, he had no concern of capture. He tied the sack full of money to his saddle and formed a cigarette with thick, dulled fingers that were calm.

'That damn bank dude's mouth flopped open shore hilariously.' The clatter of Alvin Boyd's chuckle was distorted by the wind.

No fear of pursuit marred the killer's flight. He knew the ways of the sheriff's posse. They would hole up at the first ranch. That was why he had held off until the storm broke, then rode into town and stuck up the bank. A one-man job, cleverly planned, cold-bloodedly executed. The lives he had taken were but tally notches on his gun, no more. He would boast about it when he got drunk.

'That other'n piled up like a stack of sticks.'

The storm whirled and groaned. The horse flowed with the wind, as he headed south for Indian Territory. A man could hole up there and get plenty drunk. Grub in the cabin. Wood enough for a month. Hay a-plenty, a cask of moonshine liquor. When a man got hard up for company, there was Roy Powers and his wife across the river. Roy was a damn fool but he knew how to keep his mouth shut. Roy was all right. Just didn't have the guts to go out and take chances, which were all. Maybe if it wasn't for the missus, Roy might swap a hayfork for a gun and pick up some easy money. Roy's missus was just a young thing, purdy enough, so far as looks went and kind of quiet. Scared, like as not, because she wasn't used to men that had guts – but she had sense. Close-mouthed like most breed women. No damn sheriff has ever gotten anything out of Anna Powers.

It was getting dark now – black as pitch. Alvin Boyd disappeared into his buffalo coat and let his horse drift along. He rode good horses. Whenever Alvin Boyd stole a horse, he picked a good one. It was nearly a hundred miles into the Pleasant Hills. There they dropped in timbered ridges to meet the Prairie Dog Creek. To travel all night in a blizzard was only part of a man's job. The same as killing those two bank dudes and by evening tomorrow, he would be at his cabin in the Indian Territory.

'That cask will sure look good.'

Alvin Boyd liked whiskey. He liked whiskey like most men

6

like women. Liked the color of it in a glass – liked the slosh of the stuff as it trickled out of a jug into a tin cup. Talk about music – the burn of it when a man tilted a jug and drank it that away – God – what he'd give for a drink right now.

But Alvin Boyd dared not drink until he got home. Tried it once. Fell off a horse and froze both feet sleeping in the snow. Roy Powers was horse hunting and found him. Roy's missus took care of him, Roy wasn't much of a hand to drink. A few shots and Roy had a-plenty – just enough to make that fiddle talk good. 'Old Molly Hare' and 'Hell Among the Yearlings' and 'My Love Is But a Lassie.'

Alvin hadn't seen Roy and his missus since early last spring. They were the only friends he claimed. A man on the dodge can't have many friends. Not when there's a big bounty on his head. That's the way most of the boys got theirs. Trusting somebody. Hell, them fool posses never got nowhere. Milled around. And when they followed Alvin Boyd, they kept bunched. Damn right they did.

Alvin had been in Nebraska all summer – gambling some in the middle of the sheep shearers and cowpunchers. Getting drunk and eating well. Nobody was the wiser. Who would look around sheep and cow camps for an outlaw? Then he'd up and shot that Indian cowpuncher and had to drift back north into Montana again – too quickly on the trigger.

Alvin's rattling laugh broke forth again. He took out his .45 and with the nail file blade of his jack knife, he made two new notches on the gun's bone handle. That was what that Indian had taught him. He was proud of those notches. Six, all told, counting the two bank dudes. Not bad for a man of twenty-three – he'd tell Roy and his missus. Roy would grin somewhat silly. He was not scared of a man that had guts – a man that was quick on the trigger. The missus just sat and shook as if she was taken with a chill.

Into the black jaws of the canyons and draws – snow piling in till a man felt smothered, black as tar. Chilly. Give a dollar for a drink. Hell, give five dollars. Ten. There was money a-plenty in that sack. Whiskey money.

Topping out on a long ridge. Into a dawn that was the color of soiled slate. A wind that bit plumb into a man's insides – didn't just drop into a ranch or even a sheep camp for grub. There'd be no fool sign for a posse to pick up. Nobody but Roy knew of that little log cabin tucked away in a pocket of the Indian Territory – pines and brush and rocks. Grub hoarded. Shoot a whitetail buck or a yearling. What's two days without food? Make a man eat well when he got it – whiskey and meat. Good whiskey and fat meat. Halfway home now – safe as a dog in a hole.

Keep to the gorges, just under the rim of the ridges. No use sky-lining a man's self. All day. Horse getting leg weary, he tumbled into a prairie dog hole yet no harm done. Wind that shrunk a man's heart; wind that cut the hide on a man's face. Feet like ice cakes. Like the blood was dried up. God, but that whiskey sent it charging through a man's veins, though. Fill a jug and go across to Roy Powers'. A man needed talk when he'd bin alone so long. Roy would drag out the fiddle. 'Bed River Jig' or 'Blue Bottles'.

He pulled into his secreted canyon that afternoon. A frost scorched, fur clad figure, red-eyed from the wind and loss of sleep – a lone figure in a huge white world. Cold, starving, thirsting for whiskey as a man on a parched desert longs for water. With a fortune tied in saddle bags. Two new notches on the bone handle of a short-barreled Colt .45 and a laugh jingling in his throat.

Hay in the barn – Roy had put up that hay. The well above the cabin was warm. It never froze – had an iron taste to it.

Alvin Boyd watered and fed his gaunt horse. While no law

of God or man had weight with the killer, he never violated that creed of the range that orders its men to care for a horse that has carried a man. After that, he may look to his own comfort.

Alvin Boyd found the whiskey cask buried under the hay. He found a tin cup, and with a corner of his fur coat, he wiped some of the dust from inside it. Then he crouched there by the cask and drank a cup of whiskey as if the stuff were water. He sat there for better than half an hour. Drinking until the ache melted from his bones and the hunger pains left his empty stomach. Now and then, he chuckled. The horse would give a start and look around, ears erect. Alvin Boyd's laugh was unlike the laughter of any other man because there was no humor in it. More like a death rattle.

He was stable enough on his feet when he got up and went to the cabin. As steady as a man can be when he has been frozen into the saddle for a night and a day, and when he is bundled in fur coat and chaps and four buckle over-shoes.

'Fill a jug and go visit Roy Powers, to hell with cooking. Roy's missus will toss up some grub.' His cracked, frost black-ened lips split in a grin as he saw smoke coming from the Powers' cabin, across the river among the skeleton cotton-woods.

He found a jug and filled it. Then he kicked off his chaps and located a pair of snowshoes. It was as easy going by foot as it was by horseback. He threw the jug about his shoulder with a bit of rope. Then he took his carbine and fitted it into a worn buckskin sheath.

'Whiskey. Cartridges. All set.' Then he remembered the money in the saddle-bag. 'Whiskey's taken hold.' He hid the money in the hay. Then, shuffling along on his webs, he tra-versed the river to Roy Powers' place.

Even before he knocked on the door, Alvin Boyd had a feeling that something was wrong at the home of Roy Powers. Horses in the hay corral, chewed from the snow-capped stack. Gate down. No tracks around. Cattle, thin flanked and hollow-eyed, bawling for water in the lower pasture. Woodpile buried in the snow. Yet there was smoke coming from the chimney – a light inside, against the coming dusk.

'Come in!' Was that the voice of Roy Powers? Alvin could not see through the window. Frost had made the panes obscure.

Guardedly Alvin Boyd opened the door. His jug and carbine laid aside, he held his Colt in his hand, the hammer thumbed back. He kicked the door open.

For a moment, Alvin Boyd stood there, half-crouched, ready. Then he stood. The gun hammer lowered quietly and the weapon went back into its holster.

For propped up on a bunk beside the stove, one leg in rude splints, sat Roy Powers – an empty-eyed, lean cheeked, unshaven Roy.

'Alvin Boyd!' His voice was like the gruff call of a crow. But there was a prayer in its welcome, as he voiced the killer's name.

From the bedroom beyond came a broken, moaning cry – a woman's sob, a woman half-delirious with pain.

'Horse fell and busted my leg . . . About a week ago . . . Anna took care of me until she had to quit. . . . She's going to have a baby and no doctor inside a hundred miles. I reckon she'll die.'

It took Alvin Boyd some seconds to understand fully. A pint or more of unrefined whiskey on an empty stomach does not make for quiet thinking. The fact that he could retain even an appearance of his faculties proved the tough-ness of the killer.

'Sawbones, a doctor, eh?' Alvin Boyd pushed back his cap and ran rounded fingers through his shock of coarse black hair. 'Doctor? Yeah, you sure need one, don't you, Roy?'

'Not for me, Al. Anna. She's out of her head, kinda.'

'She dyin', Roy?'

'She will, I reckon. There has to be a doctor when the baby comes.'

Alvin Boyd passed his hand across his eyes. He knew nothing of childbirth. There had never been room in his killer's heart for consideration for man or woman. Life and the losing of life meant but little to him; he nodded, brown brows knit in a pensive glare. Then he stepped outside and brought in the jug.

He poured three drinks into tin cups.

'Do us all good, Roy. Then we'll kinda figure this thing out.' He took one of the cups and went into the next room.

'Hello, Anna, git outside of this. Nothin' like it to kill pain.'

Faintly, through eyes that were mere slits of red, he saw the white face of the girl. White as the pillow against the mass of blonde hair. He lifted her head and held the cup against the lips that seemed exhausted of blood.

'The throbbing . . . the pain. . . .'

'Hell, ain't it? But that drink'll do you good.'

He went back into the other room and handed Roy his cup.

'Here's luck, Roy. Down the hatch – more where that come from.'

Alvin tossed down his drink without a scowl. His brain seemed to be clearing.

'Where do you keep your pencil and paper, Roy?'

'That drawer. God, Al, if we could only do something for Anna.'

11

'Keep your boots on.' Alvin found the writing pad and pencil. He handed them to the crippled man.

'Write a note to the doctor, Roy. You knowed I don't write. Make it scary.' Alvin pulled on his cap again. 'I'll be ready by the time you git it wrote.'

'Where you going, Alvin?'

'Out to saddle up the best horse you got. I'm going for the doctor. I'll stop by the nearest ranch and have 'em send over somebody to ride herd on you.' The door banged shut behind him.

Alvin caught Roy's best horse. When he had saddled the horse, he came back inside.

'Finished that note yet?'

'Yep. But you can't make it into town, Al.'

'Hell, I can't. The storm's done quit, I knowed the road, and I aren't that drunk but I kin ride.'

He then folded the paper and put it into his pocket.

'Hang and clatter, Roy, till the sawbones gits here.' He poured some of the whiskey into an empty vinegar bottle and put the corked bottle into his overcoat. Then he filled the two cups.

'Here's how, Roy. If the kid looks like you, I'd sure feel sorry fer the critter.'

Alvin tossed down his drink and before Roy Powers could say a word, he was gone.

It was enormous hard luck; the way things had turned out for a man. When the only friend a man had was laid up with a broken leg and an unwell wife. No 'Old Molly Hare.' No fire to set by. No Roy to talk to and tell how amusing that bank dude looked when he dropped by and no hot grub, only that bottle – better drop past the cabin and fill a jug. When a man ain't slept nor eaten he'd have a jug along to keep him alive?

He stopped at his cabin long enough to fill the jug. Then

he pulled out. He rode into a nearby line camp. Two cow-punchers gaped hard at the slit eyed, chill blackened man who staggered a little when he walked.

'Roy Powers is in a bad way. Busted a laig. His missus is dyin'. I'm ridin' fer a sawbones. One of you boys git over there and look after things.'

He gobbled some meat and beans and gave them a shot out of his jug. One of the cowpunchers was getting ready for the trip to Roy's. Alvin Boyd scrambled back into the saddle and rode on.

The storm had stopped. The stars sparkled like white flashes against the clear sky. The moon pressed up over the jagged ridges. Alvin Boyd swayed a little as he rode, half asleep, half awake, back along the trail to town.

He took some tobacco and rubbed it into his eyes to sting them open. Now and then, he took a drink from the jug. Not as big a drink as he wanted. Just enough to keep a man alive, that food made a man sleepy. A paunch full of meat always made a man sleepy. Enormous hard luck that a man couldn't get off and lie down for a few minutes. In a few hours, he'd be frozen stiff as a stick – hadn't he frozen his feet that way? Wouldn't he die there if only Roy came by? Hell, he was paying Roy back right now. A man paid his debts that way. It took guts, too. But when a man has one friend on earth, he'd be a hell of a kind of man not to lend a hand. It took guts. Something Roy didn't have. Roy was a chicken-hearted cuss. With his wife and his fiddle. Never took a chance. Never would get nowhere – like a cow pasture. Well, no man had ever sawed-off Alvin Boyd's horns. No fence made ever held him. No jail, neither. Never been caught. Those as tried had come across some hard luck. Have a drink. Damn that cork! A man's hands stiff and frozen, there she comes. Good whiskey. Thawed a man's belly. Fighting whiskey.

Alvin Boyd's laugh irritated on the silence of the winter

13

night. There would be fighting a plenty if a man run into that fool posse. Alvin took a beaded buckskin pouch and put into it the note to the sawbones. Then he fastened the pouch around his neck outside his coat. He moved with a steadfast, listless precision. He lost one of his gloves, the right glove, then put the other glove on his right hand, leaving the left one naked. Alvin Boyd's right hand was his gun hand.

Out of the hills and onto the main road to town. Daylight now. Sleepy. Nodding off in the saddle and riding that horse as if he owned him. Paying off the only debt he owed to his only friend.

Yonder was Prairie Dog Creek. With a belly full of meat, he was heading for a safe place to sleep it off.

Alvin never killed a wolf. Hell, he was a wolf, himself – a lone wolf. A killer. No rabbit, like Roy Powers, whining over a busted leg. Alvin Boyd rode alone. What would he do if he had a slug in him and had to scratch it out with a jack knife? Alvin Boyd had done that.

What's that coming yonder? Horse riders – a dozen or more, posse men more than likely, time for a drink – a big one this time. No sip. Been holding off. Waiting.

'Here's to me! I'm lookin' at you, boys!' Alvin Boyd's throaty voice carried a note of triumph. 'Here's to lookin' at you across gun sights!' And he let the burning stuff slosh down his throat.

A rifle bullet buzzed past Alvin Boyd's head. He mocked the sharpshooter with a roar of disdain and, flipping aside the jug, pulled his carbine and rode at a run straight for the men.

A barrage of bullets met his rush. Alvin Boyd's horse tumbled, shot between the eyes. Alvin tried to kick his feet from the stirrups. It was too late. Horse and man crashed together. A droning pain shot through the killer's leg. That leg was pinned under the dead weight of the horse. Bullets whizzed and buzzed by him. Alvin Boyd emptied his carbine. Two of the posse felt the blazing sting of the outlaw's bullets. Alvin pulled his six-gun – the .45 that had taken a deadly toll of human life. His thumb provoked the hammer.

'Come and git it! Come on, you damn fool law dogs!'

Black lips exposed tobacco-stained teeth. Slit eyes puffed up almost shut. It took guts.

Something white hot wounded Alvin Boyd's chest. He hardly felt it. Above the flat spat of rifles in the dawn, sounded the joyless laugh of Alvin Boyd, a cackle that sounded like the death rattle. Thumbing the hammer of an empty gun – then the exhausted head dropped back into the snow. Alvin Boyd, killer, was dead.

The last of the whiskey sloshed out of the uncorked jug into the trail.

'He must have got drunk, blind drunk, and lost his way,' a posse member said.

The sheriff pulled the dead outlaw clear of the horse. Dourly victorious, the graying old law officer inspected the body of the killer. Then he opened the pouch and found the note.

As he read it, there in the sunrise of that winter morning, the cordial glow of triumph cooled. He turned to a man who carried a small black bag instead of a gun.

'This is for you, Doc. Seems you're wanted down on the creek. The Powers' place.' He handed over the note. Then he turned to his men.

'Handle Alvin Boyd with ease, boys. Though he rode alone, seems like he had at least one friend. He came back for a purpose, to do the only respectable thing he ever done in his life. Roy Powers' wife is about to give birth. Alvin Boyd comes to get Doc. So handle him easy.'

CHAPTER 1

Asa Boyd had his initial glimpse at the town of Alcove Springs through the unfriendly uneasiness of the late spring shower which came down sideways out of the icy-cloaked, high country to the north. In what had qualified as sleep, he had spent last night sprawled in a round-backed chair in the soiled barroom of the old stage station at Newport, some thirty or so miles to the south. The cash he had spent this morning for an oily, nearly tasteless breakfast, served by a surly half-breed with a knife-scarred face, was the last money he had to his name. That had been some time ago. Now he knew hunger again, and the cold harshness which came from riding fatigued miles into the mouth of this wind-driven, unyielding rainstorm.

His slicker was worn, the life long since gone out of its once bright color. And though it was fastened to his chin, the rain's penetrating condensation had worked through in numerous places and laid a moist, miserable touch across both his shoulders and chest and down the shrinking, tense muscles in the deep of his slender stomach. Water in a steady waterfall emptied from the slovenly soaked brim of his hat. Twice in the past hour he had tried to achieve the prudent ease of a cigarette, but between the rain and the troublesome wind and the scrabbling of his cold and rigid fingers, weak papers had torn and tobacco had blown away. So he cursed in exhausted hatred and let it go at that.

The storm's murk was hastening the end of the day and lights from Alcove Springs were beginning to show. A train toot howled in solitude and a five-car freight went grumbling and reverberating to the east. The aroma of coal smoke and steam floated on the wind. Hefty also was another aroma, the unpleasant smell of wet cattle pens and loading yards.

Boyd put his skinny and exhausted paint across the tracks and reined into the end of a street that pushed jaggedly westward. He rode along this at a deliberate, plodding gait, the stride of a horse and a man both fully travel worn. There were scarce active signs of life about – just a rig or two and a reedy sprinkling of trail ponies and there along the hitch rails, heads down and patient, hindquarters turned to the wind's wet and irritating pressure. Down the street two silhouettes showed fleetingly, moving from one doorway to dip into another, and the resonance of a man's restless, swearing grievance floated back.

On the south side of the street a two-storey building lifted gaunt, square shoulders. A porch ran the full length of this, its roof a balcony for the second story. An out-jutting joist carried a swinging sign, which creaked thinly as the wind jostled it. Asa reined up under the sign, squinting against the drive of the rain as he spelled out the words in the uncertain, fading light.

BRINKLEY BLACKWELL
GENERAL MERCHANDISE

Boyd nodded to himself, put the paint onto the hitch rail, and swung stiffly from his saddle. He stood for a moment with a hand against the paint's wet flank, steadying himself until his numbed feet got full feel of the sodden earth. Just beyond the paint was a spring wagon and team, the bed of the wagon covered with a tied-down tarp. One corner of this had worked itself free and was flapping wildly in the howling wind.

Asa's glimpse met the wagon, moved on, then came directly back. The tarp, soaked from the storm, had drooped down, pensively outlining something that lay under it. There was a ghastly idea in that outline. Boyd moved in for a closer look. A draught of wind grabbed the loose corner of the tarp, warped it, and hurled it back. A booted foot was disclosed, the toe pointing upward and out in a way appallingly noteworthy.

It was a jarring find and a dreary introduction to this town of Alcove Springs. Asa Boyd moved back a step and lifted his head, his eyes searching the long reach of the suddenly long and dark street. Gravity burned in his deep-set eyes and his lips thinned out with sudden weight. He turned and ascended the low steps of the porch and for the first time in the long, tedious run of the day, found cover from the deluge.

The door of the store opened and four people exited. Two were men, one a massive figure in a hip length canvas coat, the other shorter, on the firm side, bald in a vest and shirt sleeves. The other two were women; both stood draped from chin to ankles in yellow slickers. The woman closest to him was settling a flat-crowned Stetson resolutely on her head and pulling the throat string tight against the whip of the wind. The firm man was in conflict.

'Wish you'd change your mind, Mattie. It'd be a long drive out to the ranch with Sara on a night like this, even if the wagon was empty.'

Neither woman responded to this, both moved out to the edge of the porch. The massive man in the canvas coat now

18

added his bit.

'Just speak up, Miss Roberts, and I'll have Carson Bird drive you both home.'

The closest woman turned then, and the thin, golden glow of the store lights reached through the open door. Asa Boyd, standing silently there to one side, saw that draining and paleness lay in the women's cheeks, and when the one called Mattie spoke he heard a voice that was low and freighted with a tautness that told of sentiments under tight rein.

'Sara and I will be just fine. We all will ride home together. And if there was another point of supply within reason, neither I nor any of us would ever show in this god-awful town again. You've been promising a better town, but it hasn't changed a bit. It is still the same murderous hole, and Missouri Akridge still owns most of it. Owns its outlaws and what we have for law as well!'

Both men shifted restlessly under the bitter lash of her words. The one in the canvas coat gave a rather blustering answer. 'Now that's hardly fair, Miss Roberts. Brinkley Blackwell here, and me – we're both mighty sorry about Seaborn Jones. But truth be told, he forced the trouble and the gunplay. On the spot witnesses swear that Cooper Warlow shot only in defense of hisself. And I can't hold a man for that, right?'

'Cooper Warlow!' There was a rising note of ragged and loosening emotion from the other woman – and for the first time, Asa could hear she was younger. 'A cheap and crooked man! It's the same old story, the same shameless excuse. You'd have me believe that all of Alcove Springs is sorry, wouldn't you!'

Mattie reached out to the younger woman. 'What good does it do to talk to these two? When a man is shot down just because he wouldn't stand for being robbed by a filthy thug?

But Missouri Akridge and the men he owns are never at fault, are they? Oh no, of course not! So they go on cheating and killing and getting away with it!'

She seemed to choke up, for she pushed a slender hand to her throat. Brusquely she whirled, went down the steps in a swift rush, bowed under the hitch rail, and pulled at the halter ropes of the spring wagon team. A second later she and the younger woman were up on the seat of the rig, a brake rod clanged and wailed, and then the wagon rolled out and moved down the street, turning tersely to the left and vanishing into a crossway.

The rain continued to beat down, the store sign swayed in the wind and squeaked its depressing grievance. The massive man in shirt sleeves cleared his throat inhospitably. 'Fifteen miles in weather like this – and a dead man riding in the bed of the wagon. Boykin, those girls got more courage than most of the men in this town. Mattie's right, too. This goddamn town is getting harder to swallow every day. I suggest you have a damned square talk with Missouri Akridge about his dog, Mr Cooper Warlow.'

Samuel Boykin shrugged his indifference and spat out into the rain-soaked street. 'I'm running this here town the way most people want it run, you included, Brinkley. You love the smell and sight of money just like most men, maybe more. I aim to keep this town and our pockets full of money and if I have to play to men like Cooper Warlow and Missouri Akridge, so be it.'

The storekeeper folded his arms, hugged himself against the dank chill while he stared along the deepening gloom of the street. He spoke with a slow soberness that had troubled thoughts behind it.

'And none of what you just said has anything to do with Cooper Warlow shooting Seaborn Jones, a rider from one of the biggest spreads in the area. You know damn well, Boykin, before the trail herds ever stopped here, this town of Alcove Springs had to live off the trade that came from that spread. And when the trail herds from the south stop heading our way – and that will be sooner rather than later – then Alcove Springs will be right back depending on Miss Roberts' ranch for trade. The folks from up there are our past and our future, make no mistake about that fact.'

'Could be, I reckon, some truth to your words,' agreed Boykin. 'But I'm more worried about the here and now, rather than the future, as if we poke the wrong men, neither of us will have a future to worry about. Seaborn Jones forced the situation. He lost some money to Warlow then stood and called him a cheat. Them fellas over in the saloon will attest to the fact that Seaborn went for his gun first but just wasn't fast enough for Warlow.'

'I wish Seaborn had done this town a favor and been faster,' Blackwell said drily. 'I don't doubt a bit that Cooper Warlow was cheating. The man is no good.'

Boykin shrugged again. 'I don't know anything about him being a cheat. But I do know that this latest incident is no fault of mine or yours, for that matter. For I can't be on duty night and day and be in all places all the time. I mean, iffen I was there when this started, maybe I could have headed it off before it all went south. Who knows for sure? If you and Miss Roberts or the rest of the town want me to tighten things up around here, I will need help.'

'Yeah, yeah, I know,' Blackwell said. 'If the right man comes along, Sam – you'll have him. But it's not goin' to be easy finding a man who takes that sort of work and who is capable of performing the duties admirably.'

'Yes, I am well aware of that,' Samuel Boykin agreed. 'As things stand now, I'm doing my best, you know that. I am not a young man anymore. I can't stand up to some of these punchers like I used to. I got other things to tend to.'

From the far eastern end of the street where the majority of the town's lights glowed like golden shallow beams in the eyes of a cornered mountain lion, lights advertising bars and deadfalls, there lifted a high-pitched, harsh, drunken shout, followed by the leaden, compact bang of a gunshot. Boykin whirled around – impressively for a man his size Asa thought – and listened for a second, then dropped sharply down the store steps and set off towards the noise spouting frank, acerbic words in the night air.

The storekeeper stared after Boykin, then said again, 'This godforsaken town!' He turned and stamped inside the store.

Asa Boyd followed him in, stopping just inside the door. Water ran off his drenched slicker and shone wetly in the light of the store's four hanging lamps. Boyd took off his hat, whipped it back and forth, scattering more water. Brinkley Blackwell turned with a professional, though impersonal, smile.

'What can I do for you, stranger?'

Boyd unbuttoned his slicker, shrugged out of it, dropped it to the floor. He thrust his hands under his armpits to dry them. Then, from an inner pocket, he brought out a crumpled envelope and extended it to the storekeeper, who looked at it, took out the enclosed paper and skimmed through it with just a fleeting look. Then his eyes came back to this rangy, storm-whipped man with a quickening interest.

'Have we met before?'

'Not that I can recall,' Asa replied.

The storekeeper shook his head. 'Um . . . you sure remind me of someone. . . Anyways . . . what is your business with this Alvin Boyd?'

'Well, that'd be my business and no one else's.'

'Don't get yourself all lathered up . . . under the circumstances, I've got to make sure. No offense intended, young

22

man. But when you set out to fulfill the trust of a dead man, you owe it to his memory to be true.'

'Sure.' Asa tipped his head slightly.

'How did you know this Boyd?' asked Blackwell. 'For instance, can you describe what he looked like? What sort of things was he into?'

'He stood about as tall as me, I reckon . . . thereabouts,' Asa Boyd said. 'He was fairly lean, not one to be kept inside or caged. He had brown hair, green eyes, and when last I saw him, he remarked on his love of whiskey. He was twenty-five. His laugh was a tad strange, as it did not seem genuine. He often got himself into trouble, usually over women, whiskey or cards. He could handle a gun decent enough.'

'All right . . . you obviously knew the man. There ain't much to turn over to you. The law could have confiscated all his money and stuff, they had the right. The amount was so paltry that the law just let it be. Of course, they did not find the money he had stolen from the bank . . . least not on him. . . .'

'The money he presumably stole from the bank, you mean.'

'Yeah . . . sure.' The storekeeper went over to the safe, opened it, and brought out a compact canvas sack which appeared to be empty.

'There it is, all thirteen dollars of it, the amount he had on him when he. . . .' Blackwell paused to look at Asa. '. . .well, minus the cost of his burial. I do not know if he had any kin. You related to him? Cousin? A brother perhaps?'

Asa Boyd said nothing.

Blackwell went to untie the sack while he spoke. 'You can count it to make sure.'

'Not necessary,' said Boyd in his terse, quiet way. 'I thank you for holding on to it for him.'

Blackwell watched Boyd snatch the sack. He was watching

23

a lanky, big-shouldered man who had that certain roughness that dense, heavy bones supplied. This same roughness tarnished a face that was wide across the cheekbones. This man was a little tall, fairly muscular, average build, except for the shoulders, short, curly brown hair, and eyes that were large and green.

Boyd spoke again, brusquely. 'There is another favor to ask of you, Mr Blackwell. Tell me, who shot Alvin Boyd?'

Blackwell's reply held a thread of abruptness. 'Well . . . I wasn't there . . . I don't rightly know . . . you see the posse had gone after him . . . and. . . .'

Boyd considered this for one long moment, his large eyes taciturnly ruminating. 'So not one man came back to town with the posse celebrating the shooting of Alvin Boyd . . . supposed bank robber and killer?'

Blackwell raised himself to the counter, sat there for some little time thinking.

'Perhaps,' he said at the moment. 'It was a crazy night, if I recall. Well, the day started when Alvin entered the bank and in the process of robbing it . . . killed one of the tellers . . . must've thought he'd gone for a gun. He rode out of town after that.'

'What happened to the other riders who'd come in with Alvin?' Asa asked.

Blackwell shrugged. 'After the shooting, no one recalled him riding in with any others. Maybe they scattered or chickened out before the robbery.'

Asa shook his head. 'There were other men involved. Alvin did not plan and execute this all on his own. Now about the posse and Alvin's death '

'As I said,' Blackwell went on, 'it was a crazy day and night, so much going on. I was helping the sheriff hand out rifles to the posse men. I had to close up the store for regular customers, you see. I went out on the porch and heard somebody running up-street later the next night, that would be west or close enough, as I recall. It was one of those snowy, frigid nights. Alvin had holed up at the Powers' place, it seemed. It was a few hours later that they – the posse – came back with the body. Two of the posse men carried Alvin into the store and waited for the doc. You see, back at the Powers' place, old Doc Perry was helping Mrs Powers deliver a baby. It was some time before he came back to town.'

Blackwell stared at the floor, fretting over the image the memory brought with it. He went on, 'Doc Perry needed only to glance at Alvin Boyd to pronounce him dead. That was it.'

'You say he didn't ride into town with some men, that Alvin Boyd rode in alone, robbed the bank and in the process shot and killed a teller in cold blood?'

'That's what happened . . . so they say,' Blackwell replied.

'They? Who would that be? Missouri Akridge?'

Blackwell tightened his lips and pulled at them with thumb and forefinger. 'I don't know about that. . . .'

'And this Akridge, he has a crew of men that do whatever it is that he wants, I bet.'

'I reckon, but. . . .' Blackwell was searching for words. 'Mr Akridge is a businessman, owns most of the town and does a lot of good things for the town. . . .'

Asa went silent, his face hopelessly reticent. 'And I suppose it was mostly Akridge's men who made up this posse.'

Blackwell became motionless, not sure if any movement could be construed as an admission of sorts.

Asa Boyd's head came up and his voice ran harsh. 'It wasn't just the money that brought me here to Alcove Springs. Alvin Boyd was dear to me. So maybe I will stick around and if I look long and hard enough, I may find some holes in the story of his robbing, killing and being killed by a posse.'

'Now we don't want no trouble around here,' Blackwell said. 'Understanding how you feel about your ... um ... friend. But I wouldn't know where or how to tell you to start.'

Eyes squeezed with thought, Asa mused on this. He stared into his irritated thoughts for a spell, then ran his glance along the store shelves. 'I'll be around for a time and will need some new clothes. And would you recommend a place where I could find a room?'

'Ben Worrill's Spring View Hotel is as good as the other in town.' Blackwell looked Asa up and down with a skillfully measuring eye and began laying out the required clothes from well-stocked shelves.

'These are on me ... mister. . . ?'

'Casady ... Asa Casady, and I don't like handouts,' Boyd said, giving the man his mother's maiden name. Now that his hands were dry and somewhat warm again, he was able to properly twist up his long-denied cigarette. Through a mouthful of smoke, he spoke slowly. 'I was able to hear some of what that Boykin fella had to say outside. I take it he's the town sheriff? He was asking for a man to help him out, and you admitted he could use one. Still feel the same about that statement?'

This brought Blackwell up, straight and startled. He sensed there was more to this stranger. 'Why, you interested?'

'I wouldn't be askin' if I weren't.'

Again, Brinkley Blackwell considered the lanky, lofty stranger with the large green eyes. 'You've the look of being able to take care of yourself, like you have some experience with that. I reckon you've had some gunplay in your past.' The storekeeper paused. 'But I must warn you, it's a low paying, thankless job. For no matter which way you go, you'll be on someone's wrong side. There is a certain manner this town is run, and at times they can seem a bit confusing. Then again there's always the chance that some crazy trail puncher might—'

'I know all that already,' cut in Asa. 'This ain't my first go around in towns like this. But the fact is I need a job . . . if I can get it, that is.'

'You're askin' the wrong person. Besides it is a job that you most likely will regret, iffen you were to get it. From what you've said, your big interest is running down the events and untimely death of your friend, Alvin Boyd. You figure that being a deputy will allow you that?'

'That's a thought. I'd have legitimate entry into every dive and deadfall in town without arousing suspicion, as if I weren't I'd just be some strange drifter poking his nose into the town's affairs.'

The storekeeper nodded gravely. 'That is true. I will speak with the sheriff first thing tomorrow morning. It's not up to me, mind you. That is all I can do.'

Asa gathered up his clothes and wrapped a new slicker around them. 'I thank you for the loan of the clothes. I intend to pay you back shortly.' He nodded to the store-keeper, then turned for the door. He stopped. 'I reckon, for the time being, it might be wise not to mention my connection to Alvin Boyd. At least not until I get settled.'

'That does sound like the prudent thing to do,' granted Blackwell.

'Once I get settled, it won't matter much. It might even start shedding some light on the truth.'

'In this town it is smart to be silent about a good many things, Mr Casady. And for that reason, it wouldn't be wise for Carson Bird and me to seek you out at the hotel. You'll be putting your horse – that paint – up at the livery, I trust? Well, after you've had your supper I suggest you make your way down to Carson's layout to check where your horse is kept. Then we can call it a night.'

There was a stairway at one end of the store, leading up to the second storey. Now, as Asa Boyd – Casady – turned to leave, steps sounded and a womanly figure moved off the stairs and out where the store lights could shine on her.

'Dinner's ready,' the woman called.

Asa took his cue and left the store. Outside, the wind was still shoving a hefty way around, but the rain had relaxed to a light shower. Asa led his soaked and exhausted paint over to the livery stable, arranged for the care of the animal, then trudged through the mud to the Spring View Hotel.

Ben Worrill bowed his head. 'Bathroom is at the end of the hall. I am sorry that I will not have hot water until morning, my boy has gone for the night. Going to be a guest with us long?'

Asa seemed to consider this possibility with deep thought. After which he shrugged nonchalantly. 'We shall see.'

In the room, Asa opened his warbag and produced a heavy Colt pistol that had been swathed in an oily cloth. He inspected the weapon, spun the cylinder a few times, and then from a partly emptied box of cartridges, filled five chambers of the weapon before lowering the hammer on the empty sixth chamber. He then slipped the pistol inside the waistband of his pants, pushing it more to his left side. He fell asleep on the bed, atop the sheets, as not to soil them before he could get cleaned up in the morning.

CHAPTER 2

Carson Bird, the owner of Alcove Springs' one and only livery barn and corrals, was a sinewy, wiry gentleman with graying hair and shrewd, even eyes. He and Brinkley Blackwell were huddled over a small, cast-iron stove in a corner room of the stable. The smell of wet hay and fresh manure hung in the air. There was a table, a bunk, and a couple of chairs, all of which had seen better days. A low-turned lamp on the table fought the gloom back moderately. A battered tea kettle hissed and whistled atop the stove.

There was a hint of reservation in Carson Bird's handshake at Blackwell's introduction, and in the dimly lit room, Asa could feel the man's glance measuring him carefully.

'Now that we are past the particulars,' said Bird, 'Brinkley here tells me you're willing to take on with us as a deputy, Mister . . . Casady, is it?'

Asa nodded his response.

Bird backed up to the stove again, with his hands behind him. 'Well, I wouldn't have thought we'd get someone here in Alcove Springs as a deputy. But I will take a tad more convincing if I'm to give my stamp of approval.'

Asa's eyes squeezed tight as he eyed the livery man. 'Meaning what exactly?'

Carson Bird seemed to settle himself more firmly on his spread feet. 'Mr Casady, me and Brinkley here have seen this town of Alcove Springs grow since it was nothing more than a few poorly built houses. We would like to feel that we are part of the foundation of this town. We – I mean I know I would – like to think the town was built for decent, hard-working folk. I would like this town to keep growing and be around with the same principles, long after I'm gone.'

The livery owner freshened his pipe, then struck a match to it as he continued.

'Now I think I can claim to being a practical man and no one has been able to tell me different . . . no woman, either.' He paused to snicker at his own joke. 'But there are those who have come into our town who offer it neither honesty, hard work, nor decency. Men like Missouri Akridge, for one, whose purposes are more in the shadows. I'm not afraid to speak my mind about him, and he knows this. I don't have the time or patience for men like him and neither should anyone else in this town.'

Carson Bird had been speaking with his head slightly bent and his eyes fixed on a corner of the shadowed room. Now he straightened and his glance struck Asa Casady squarely.

'If it should occur, Mr Casady, that you were out and 'bout wearing a tin star, would you be willing to stand toe to toe on the principles of this town, or would your only concern be the working out of your own revenge?'

Asa turned and stared hard at Brinkley Blackwell, who spoke quietly.

'Believe I told you that Carson here heard the shot that killed Alvin Boyd. It is apparent to us both that you are kin to him. No use in denying it.' The man paused. 'Not to worry, Carson and I will keep that a secret, as we liked the way Alcove Springs was before Missouri Akridge and others of his ilk showed up.'

Asa nodded curtly and turned back to Carson Bird. 'You got a marshal here – that big man Boykin. What's keeping him from goin' after Akridge?'

'He's an Akridge man,' snapped Bird. 'Oh, not all open or even consciously. There have been times when we thought we glimpsed a good bone in Boykin. But there is clearly a line in him, established by Akridge, of course. He has a different opinion of Akridge and Emory Dahlberg than most of Alcove Springs. He has shot more excuses about them then he has bullets at outlaws.'

'When I came into town this evening I saw a dead man in the back of a spring wagon,' Asa said. 'That an example of the point you are making?'

'Exactly,' put in Blackwell. 'Seaborn Jones, a Roberts ranch hand, was one of Mattie Roberts' riders. He ran into a crooked card game over at the Silver Saloon and was killed when he objected. Old Sam Boykin claims that witnesses to the shooting will swear that Seaborn pulled his gun first – and perhaps he did. If the game had been on the up and up in the first place, none of this would have happened. I knew Seaborn to be a fair man, an affable man, not the type of man to start trouble, especially with the likes of a man like Cooper Warlow.'

'Then it sounds as if me becoming deputy to this Boykin wouldn't be the best,' Asa pointed out. 'And if I went against Akridge or one of his men, if they didn't kill me then he would probably just fire me.'

'Not so fast,' said Carson Bird quickly. 'Once Sam brings you on and you show you can handle the job, he can't just fire you without the backing of the town's board, which Brinkley and I are proud members of.'

'Why not just get rid of Boykin as sheriff then?' Asa suggested bluntly.

31

'Now that would solve a lot of our issues, wouldn't it?' acknowledged Bird. 'And it is something we've considered, believe you me. But he'd make quite the fuss over that, I'm convinced. Akridge and Dahlberg would no doubt bring in fancy lawyers from back East or something. But right now, having a sheriff is better than not having one. If you get what I'm saying?'

'You're sayin' if I can prove myself as deputy, you may just be for me replacing Boykin.'

'The boy is quick,' replied Carson Bird. 'And that we shore see, Mr Casady.'

Asa's cigar had gone out. He touched a match to the stove and when it lit up in flame, he relit the cigar. He considered the situation soberly, and saw with perfect clarity what he'd be getting himself into. This town of Alcove Springs was obviously divided, the sound and decent element on one side, the darker elements on the other. And he would be getting the dubious honor of placing a target squarely on his back or more aptly – a star on his chest.

'This could all blow up in all of our faces,' Asa murmured, speaking his thought aloud, a sardonic note in his words.

'True,' nodded Blackwell.

'Yes,' added Bird, quick to understand. 'It will no doubt be dangerous. I won't lie to you and tell you otherwise. We can't make you accept the position. I do believe you have your own path as well to handle, a path that could create more danger for you.'

Asa's words hardened. 'And when the two paths cross, will I have any backing or would I be left to fend for myself?'

'If you ride on the side of what is good for this town, you'll have the backing. But I fear this other path may lead you into the darkness that is starting to enter this town. Remember, all men like Brinkley and I care about is seeing that this town thrives for generations to come. I don't want to sound callous, Mr Casady, but we are not backing your vengeance.'

'Of course not.'

The livery owner and storekeeper exchanged glances.

Asa began to pace slowly as he spoke. 'I might have to use some force.'

'No might about it,' agreed Blackwell. 'With Akridge's men, that is all but given.'

'If the situation demands force or you being rough, use it – show just as much as is necessary, but don't lose control. We will be there to back you.'

'OK,' Asa said. 'I am good, if you are?'

A quick, small smile touched Carson Bird's lips and his hand shot out. 'Young man, I think we understand each other. From what I'd seen of Alvin Boyd – and if you are anything like him – I liked him. Sorry about what happened to him, too. I, for one, do not believe all that was said about him. So I wish you success in your quest. Beyond that, if you'll put a little steel into the running of Alcove Springs, I'm sure we all will be happier.'

Carson Bird turned to Brinkley Blackwell. 'It'll be your task, Brinkley, to sell this man Casady to Missouri Akridge and Emory Dahlberg. You have the gift of gab over me.'

'All right,' Blackwell agreed. All three men shook hands in the lamp light and agreed that the next day they would get Asa on as deputy.

CHAPTER 3

Town Sheriff Samuel Boykin's office was made up of two rooms at the corner building standing halfway along the run of the town's main street; the rear room served as his living quarters. When Asa and Blackwell came in, Boykin was seated at his desk. The lawman looked up and grumbled.

'This rain will not stop, Brinkley.'

'You speak the truth, Sam.' Blackwell nodded. 'Sam, shake hands with your new deputy, Asa. . . .' The storekeeper paused, shot a swift look at Asa. 'Asa Casady.'

Sheriff Boykin straightened in his chair, his gaze going razor-sharp as he looked Asa up and down. 'Where'd you find him?'

'He just rode in and hit me up for a job. Asked if there was an opening for that kind of work and I informed him there might be.'

Boykin's handshake was fleeting, yet cordial. He eyed Asa with a certain grimacing guardedness however. 'Sounds very fortunate. Is there more to this than what you have told me, Brinkley?'

'Sure,' Asa chimed in. 'I was at the store last night, in the driving rain, when I overheard you, Mr Blackwell here and some women talking before they rode off with a dead man in the back of their wagon.'

Boykin settled back in his chair, still studying Asa. 'I am in need of a deputy, all right,' he conceded. 'What kind of experience do you have?'

'Nothing with the law. But I'm a quick study.' Boykin still showed a shrewd indecision, something that Blackwell picked up on and he spoke frankly.

'Sam, you've been whining about having some help. Now either you need help or you don't. If you do, then here you have an able-bodied man, willing to learn. I don't want to hear you whining about being overworked any longer. So – what's your answer?'

There was a bite in Blackwell's words that made Boykin's heavy face redden. 'Well, can I have a moment to collect my thoughts, geez, Brinkley. A man does not buy a horse by just looking at it.' Again that air of hesitation hung before them all. 'I mean, it is my and this office's reputation on the line. I need to know more about this man . . . wouldn't you agree?'

'You mean Missouri will want to approve your hiring of him?' Blackwell noted.

Boykin nodded and straightened more. 'Of course, Mr Akridge's counsel is always warranted in such matters. After all he has done so much for the town.'

'Fine,' said Blackwell, 'will Mr Dahlberg also be needed on this hire?'

Boykin nodded again.

'They'll be at their regular game, I reckon?' Blackwell asked.

The sheriff stood, put on his canvas coat, blew out the lamp, and led the way into the street. Now the rain and the wind had diminished, and the air was dense with saturated dampness that lifted from the puddled earth and bit at a man's bones. Boykin hurried his charging stride toward the grandest looking saloon along Main Street.

Here was the flamboyance to go with the name. A long

bar, close-packed gaming tables, and a cleared area at the far end where several dance-hall girls relaxed minus partners, and where a slim, black-haired, thin-faced man with oddly ashen skin sat around a piano.

Boykin shook a nod to a bartender. 'Business slow, eh, Eli?'

'Dead as a wagon wheel,' was the unexciting comeback. 'Might as well close up for the night. What can I do for ya?'

'Missouri,' said Boykin.

'He's out back. Him and the two Dahlbergs. Nathan Crewell and Cooper Warlow.'

Boykin went to a rear door, knocked twice, then once more, before opening it, and led the way through without waiting for a summons. Five men were at a poker table under the circular cone of brightness ebbing down from an overhead lamp. Boykin focused his words at one of the players, a touch of regret in his manner.

'My apologies for the interruption, Mr Akridge, but this won't take long. Brinkley Blackwell has dug up a deputy for me, and I wanted to get your opinion of the man. If he suits you, he will suit me too.'

Brinkley Blackwell took a step to the front. 'This is Asa Casady, gentlemen. As you probably recall, we've been promising Boykin a night man for some time, and Casady is willing to take the position. And Casady, starting from here and around the table is Ferrill Dahlberg, the son, next Cooper Warlow, Emory Dahlberg, the father, Nathan Crewell, and Missouri Akridge.'

Asa gave a quick, measuring glance at the five men. Ferrill Dahlberg was a short, stocky, curly-haired young man, good-looking in a florid way, but with a somewhat spoiled, sarcastic-looking mouth and eyes that carried a hot restlessness in their depths. Cooper Warlow was plainly all gambler and most likely a gunfighter, a neutral-looking sort, without a shade of expression on his pale, locked features.

Like his son, Emory Dahlberg was stocky. He was red-faced, bald. He chewed wetly on the remnants of a cigar, the juice of which laid its brown stain at the corners of his mouth and along the edges of his fat lips. Nathan Crewell was a riding man, with the smell of horse sweat fresh on him. His face was bony and hard and under jutting brows, his eyes seemed to have receded to a cold wariness. He badly needed a shave and lank hair hung raggedly about his shirt collar.

It was Missouri Akridge who was the dominating figure at the table. At that moment he pushed his chair back, got to his feet, and moved over to a chair that had a black, broadcloth coat hung across it. The businessman dredged a cigar from a pocket of the garment and while he nipped off the end of the cigar, lit it, and rolled it between his lips, he studied Asa Casady with small, hard, heavily-lidded eyes.

A man of average size, this Missouri Akridge owned to a certain sleek plumpness. His smooth-shaven face was unlined and on the swarthy side. His lips were full, sensuous. His hair was sleek and coal-black except for a streak of almost silver-gray which ran along the left side of his head. The contrast of this was startling, marking the man as definitely as a physical disfigurement might have, and was obviously something he was not too ashamed of. He moved with an unhurried, but soft efficiency that carried a suggestion of the feline about it. In Asa Casady's eyes, this Missouri Akridge was, on first look, a very dangerous man.

It was Ferrill Dahlberg who spoke first. 'Your regular trade, Mr Casady – is it wearing a badge?'

'I've never been a lawman before. But I feel I can handle the position, or I wouldn't have asked for it.'

'Maybe,' went on young Dahlberg, 'you're one of the breed who fancies himself with a gun – and is always looking for an excuse to use it?' There was a caustic bite in both the tone and the word choices.

Asa narrowed his eyes. This young man had a way with him that got under his skin. Asa held his tongue, and kept his temper in check, though his answer was curt.

'I can use a gun when I need to, but using it is not my preferred option, if that's what you are saying.'

'And what would a saddle-tramp like you know about being a lawman?'

This brought a raw harshness leaping out of Asa. 'I ain't claiming to know much. As I told the sheriff, I am a quick learner. Who are you to suggest otherwise?'

Now it was the elder Dahlberg who spoke quickly. 'Just a minute, Mr Casady – let it lay, let it lay! And Ferrill, you keep that damned sarcastic tongue of yours to yourself. Quit trying to throw your weight around. Now I, for one, like this man Casady's style. And Brinkley, you must like it, too, or you wouldn't be recommending him. Missouri, what do you make of this fella?'

However he felt, Missouri Akridge was not expanding on it to any great length. He shrugged his sleek shoulders with a callous indifference, giving the impression that this whole thing was more or less boring to him. When he finally answered, his voice was purring and smooth as his face.

'Seems fine to me. Anything to keep Boykin from crying around how badly he's overworked. We can,' he added, with a certain soft ruthlessness, 'always get rid of this fellow Casady if he doesn't work out.'

'Well, OK then,' said the elder Dahlberg, 'I guess that settles this matter.'

'Then let's get the game goin' again,' snapped Ferrill Dahlberg.

Samuel Boykin, feeling that this shut them out, jerked his head toward the door and led the way. As they emerged into the big barroom, Brinkley Blackwell dropped a hand on

Asa's arm, murmuring, 'Good luck, Mr Casady.'

Asa showed him a small smile. 'Thanks, I may need it. How come them don't invite you into their game?'

Blackwell's answering smile was dry, a little wintry. 'I'm not interested and they know that. Oh, I can enjoy a friendly game of draw for low stakes where nobody gets hurt, win or lose. But those fellows don't play for those types of stakes. Besides, I've a business to run. Right now I've some books to work over before I can go to bed.'

Outside, Blackwell headed to his store, while Asa and Boykin stopped at the sheriff's office, where the lawman got the lamp going again. He waved Asa to a chair, took the one behind the desk, and settled into it with a grunting sigh.

'Sometimes I wonder why any man is damn fool enough to pack a badge,' he growled. 'It's a dog's life, my boy. No matter what you do or, more importantly, don't do, you will be considered wrong. Whichever way you move, you're stepping on the toes of somebody who sets up to make sure you and everyone knows that. You're between hell and high water all the time.'

'Then,' drawled Asa, 'why not do what you figure to be the right choice and let the laws of this land sort the rest out, regardless?'

Boykin shrugged. 'That sounds good, but it ain't that easy or simple, my boy.'

'And yet you still are the sheriff.'

'That's right, I am,' agreed the lawman. 'But I'm riding law on this town because I yearn to bring sweetness and light to a lot of damn fools who wouldn't recognize such things if it hit them square in the face. This is just a job to me, a way to earn a living. And bad as it is, I prefer it to punching cattle. Better pay for one thing. Also, I eat better and sleep in a bed with a roof over my head, in good weather or bad. Which beats all hell out of crawling in and out of a wet tent along a rainy trail somewhere, as I've done plenty often in my time.'

Boykin dug around in the desk drawer, came up with a pipe which he packed, and carefully lighted. Then, through a drift of smoke, he looked at Asa with shrewd intentness.

'It'll pay you to get the picture straight, Mr Casady. There'll be times when you will have to play both sides against things that you will not agree with. It's like this. Here are certain people, for example, you will have to get along with. Like Missouri Akridge or Emory Dahlberg. Make no bones about it, these types of men will push you to the limits of your patience.'

'What about the younger Dahlberg?' questioned Asa. 'Where does he rate? I got a gut feeling about him, for whatever that's worth.'

Boykin waved a soothing hand. 'He's just a spoiled, conceited pup. As you've seen, there's a mean, vile, cynical streak in that boy. But when his old man snaps his fingers, young Ferrill will straighten up. That is an odd family. I can't remember Ferrill doing a day's work in his life. All Ferrill seems to pay any attention to is the head of the Roberts' Ranch.'

Asa, remembering a slim, slicker-draped girl about to face the long ride through the mud and muck with a dead man in the back of her wagon, stirred a little agitatedly.

'Now Brinkley,' Asa offered, 'seems to be a fair man.'

'Oh, certainly,' agreed the sheriff. 'Brinkley is all right. He's what I would call decent folk. But Brinkley's trouble is he is a daydreamer, always thinking back to the good ole days, before the railroad and what not coming to town. He doesn't admire growth.'

'And he doesn't much like men such as Akridge, huh?'

'Maybe,' shrugged the sheriff. 'The position pays $125 a month. We will work out the shift hours until it suits us both.

40

If you'd like, before you turn in for the night, I'll take you over the beat and show you what things to be mindful of.'

'That sounds great, Sheriff,' Asa said, nodding.

As they went out again and along the street, a lank figure emerged from the saloon, moved to a horse at the hitch rail, and went slogging off into the night out the western end of main street.

'Nathan Crewell,' acknowledged Boykin. 'Rough one, that fella, from what I've heard. I've never had any trouble from him, however. Friend of Missouri Akridge. If we don't give any cause to give us any trouble, best to just leave men like him and Warlow be.'

An hour or so later, Asa was back in his room in the hotel. He got the lamp lit, took off his coat. For some time, he stared at the badge on his shirt. He went for his bag, unwrapped his pistol, and took the oily cloth and began to polish the badge.

A last glance to the street outside revealed mostly darkness with limited lights strung feebly along its edges. A quiet and peaceful night, Sheriff Boykin had called it – one of the few as it was.

Asa thought of other things, of his brother Alvin, who rode away and never came back. Because this town had killed him. This town of Alcove Springs, with its bars and its deadfalls, with its predators.

Asa stirred, a hand going up to touch the newly polished badge on his shirt. His lip curled a trifle. He undressed, turned in, and was summarily asleep.

CHAPTER 4

The next morning was a fine one – as fine as anyone could have wished for. The foul weather had disappeared overnight. Lowering clouds had drifted and cleared now, with a brilliant sun glinting across the world, the sky was a deep-washed cobalt and everything seemed to gleam from the purging of the rain. As the touch of the sun grew in power, the world steamed and smoldered with vapors that lifted and melted. There was a brusqueness in the air to sting a man's lungs and send the good surge of life flowing energetically.

Asa, relishing his after-breakfast cigar, headed along the street to the livery barn, where Carson Bird stood out front, welcoming the caress of the sun. The livery owner displayed a small contained smirk and foreboding twist of his head.

'Now if I was an illogical man,' he whispered, 'I might see all of this as some sort of omen. A clear and brilliant day and you with that gleaming deputy badge. It fits you.'

'There is definitely more seriousness to this tin star,' Asa answered. 'I didn't really understand that before it was put on my chest.'

Carson Bird nodded his head again. 'Now if that beat all – Brinkley and I being correct in our measurements of you. You're a good man, of that I have little doubt. What do you think of the town's council?'

Asa took a moment to consider his words. 'I never give my thoughts on a man until I've had enough time to make a proper judgement.'

There was the sound of hoofs on drenched earth and a rider cut into the street from a road that ran into town from the direction of the Roberts' spread to the north. Asa started somewhat. The rider was the woman from his first night in Alcove Springs.

She was no longer swathed in the wet yellow slicker, but instead wore a cozily fastened buckskin coat which high-lighted the straight shape of her shoulders and the full nimble strength of her. The ends of a pale silk bandana flapped at her throat.

'Mattie Roberts!' exclaimed Carson Bird softly. 'Now what would she be wanting back in town? After all that mess with her rider, Seaborn Jones – didn't figure to see her back in town so soon.'

Asa kept quiet, watching the woman. She headed directly to Brinkley Blackwell's general store, swung down, and darted inside. Her horse had been ridden hard, as it was sucking hard for air.

It was only a moment before she and Blackwell emerged from the store. From the edge of the porch Blackwell looked up and down the street, then across to where Asa and Carson stood. He then lifted an arm towards them and beck-oned.

'Now who do you think he is calling – you or me?' asked Carson. 'Best find out.'

They went across and it was to Asa that Blackwell spoke as they approached him and the woman. 'We may have some trouble headed our way, Asa. Miss Roberts' crew is riding in after Cooper Warlow. She would like them headed off before they make it to town. I'm not sure where Sam is right at this moment, so you are the man for the job.'

Asa looked to the woman. She looked back at him with solemn, clear eyes that were shadowed with worry. Asa spoke. 'Are you tellin' me that your riders ride against your wishes?'

'Um . . . unfortunately, yes.' Her voice was soft yet provoking. 'When I returned my man – Seaborn Jones – to my ranch and after we laid him to rest, the rest were wild with anger. I pleaded with them to forget it and just move on – as Seaborn would've wanted. It was all for nothing, my ramrod – James Allum – told me what he and the men were intending to do. I argued with them. They would not listen. I rode hard and fast – taking short cuts, but they are not far behind me.'

'What are their intentions for this Cooper Warlow?'

She nodded, and her tone grew in intensity. 'One of them has a rope, already tied in a noose, and the others have picked out a tree just outside of town. They plan to drag him down the streets of the town and out to this tree where. . . .'

Asa stopped her from continuing seeing the pain on her face. 'How many are they?'

'Five.'

Asa's eyes narrowed. 'This is not goin' to be easy. Let's see if we can find the sheriff as I try to come up with some way to prevent this.' He turned and hurried away, and the woman's call followed him.

'Please – do not shoot them.'

Asa did not stop to answer her. He was preoccupied on how to stop five angry, vengeful men.

Blackwell had no idea where to find Boykin, as no one had seen the man since parting with him the day before. He first looked in the office, but it was empty. The storekeeper next set his sights on the saloon.

The barroom was showily empty, except for a single bartender and one other man – whom he did not immediately recognize. Blackwell caught the bartender's attention. 'See the sheriff – um . . . Sam . . . this morning?'

The bartender gave a slight nod indicating the back room. 'He's in there.'

Blackwell moved to the rear door, opened it, and stepped through. Boykin was there, all right. So too was Missouri Akridge, and the man Miss Roberts' men were riding to town to lynch – Cooper Warlow. Akridge was in the midst of a harsh remark. He wavered only fleetingly at the storekeeper's sudden appearance, then went on to finish what he was saying.

'Understand me, Boykin – and understand me completely! You were not hired to tell me how to run my business or affairs. Cooper Warlow is my top man. I take care of my men. Nothing more to say! Understood?'

Under the bite of Akridge's tone, Samuel Boykin's face was glowing and his eyes were morose. He turned to Blackwell with some relief. 'You need me?'

'Yeah . . . Asa is lookin' for ya,' the storekeeper said. 'Have a situation that needs your attention.'

Blackwell saw Warlow's jaw tighten and his face revealed what appeared to be rage, but it was hard to be sure as the man's eyes were cold.

Boykin was caught off guard. 'I reckon that would be the men from the Roberts' spread coming after Warlow here?'

'That'd be the situation,' Blackwell responded.

'How'd you hear about it?' the sheriff asked.

'Miss Roberts herself.'

'What in Sam Hill?' Boykin uttered. 'They're her men. Don't that beat all!'

Impatience put a rasp into Brinkley Blackwell's voice. 'These men will be here any moment, Sam. We're wastin' time, here. Best get a movin'.'

Samuel Boykin turned to Missouri Akridge with a smug smile of triumph. 'So it looks like I was right to be concerned, Missouri.'

Akridge took a cigar out, lit it with steady hands, then said, 'All I see in this is a chance for you to do the job you were hired to do, Boykin. Get on out there. I would suggest time to put into effect that new town ordinance we were discussing right now. The one that states no persons allowed in town with a gun.' The businessman smiled pessimistically through the smoke of his newly lit cigar.

Boykin turned to leave and Blackwell was on his heels, then the sheriff stopped short as Akridge's next words hit directly at him.

'If you cannot handle this, Boykin, perhaps that new deputy can.'

The lawman came fully around, eyeing this slim, dark man with an emotionlessly gaping contempt. His reply ran curt. 'I can do the job – don't you worry none, Akridge.'

He turned once more on his heel and walked out.

In the street, Samuel Boykin and Brinkley Blackwell parted ways. Boykin headed along at his lunging walk and found Asa Casady in the meanwhile. Asa moved up even with the sheriff, and it was the seasoned lawman who spoke first.

'Sounds like we have ourselves a fine mess headed our way.'

Asa grunted and nodded his response.

Boykin shot him a quick and startled glance, but said nothing more as the two continued on.

The woman, Mattie Roberts, stood waiting at the steps of Boykin's office with Carson Bird. Coming up to them, Boykin spoke with a hint of annoyed roughness.

'What in hell is goin' on with your spread, Miss Roberts?

What kind of operation you runnin' out there? Better yet, what type of men have you got riding for your brand?'

The woman flushed and her chin came up. 'They're good men, all of them, I swear, Sheriff. They wouldn't be riding here if they weren't. They liked Seaborn – heck, everyone did. His death might mean nothing to the rest of the folk around here, but it does to them . . . and to me.'

Carson Bird, who had been watching the road in from the Roberts spread, spoke with a soft dryness.

'If you got any thoughts, Sam – best be quick about them. Miss Roberts' riders are here!'

All three turned to look at the approaching riders. They rode at a measured lope, a compact group of riders showed. Samuel Boykin's heavy face pulled into a scowl.

'Just what do those damn fools figure they'll accomplish with this?'

'I believe they intend to lynch that fellow Warlow,' Asa simply replied.

Before the sheriff could respond, Asa headed for the junction of the road and the street. Behind him he could hear Boykin's heavy step and the growling mumble of the man's uneasy anger. Boykin, he decided, was showing signs of being anything but a staunch pillar to lean on.

At the junction, Asa stopped and watched the approaching riders with narrowed eyes. Sheriff Boykin came up beside him, huffing in disgust.

'Five of them – only two of us. Iffen they really are intent on lynching Warlow, not much we can do to stop them. Far as I care, they can have the louse. When Brinkley found me in the saloon I'd been trying to convince Akridge that it might be smart if Warlow went away for a spell. Neither of them would listen to me. So, I ask, why should we risk our lives for Warlow?'

Asa displayed him a sudden look, then glanced away

again, a valley of disdain rising in his throat, coming up from his gut. 'You and me are the law here, Boykin. There's either a law in Alcove Springs or there's not. Can't be both. We cannot allow men to be lynched without a proper trial.'

The riders approach was closer, with a hint of warning in their ride. Out front rode a man who was hard and immense.

'How do we stop them?' Asa questioned the sheriff.

Boykin spat and then cursed mutely, stepped out, and threw up one hand. The riders slowed from a lope to a trot, then to a walk, before coming to a stop. The big rider in the lead reined in but a few feet in front of Boykin and Asa.

'You aiming to stop us, Sheriff?' The big man's voice was as big as its owner.

Boykin was red-faced. 'Now hear me out, Allum. You know I can't allow you fellas to ride in here and lynch a man for no good reason.'

'No good reason?' Allum fired back. 'You know damn well what our reason is.' He paused and looked past the two lawmen and saw his boss. 'Had a feeling that girl would short-cut us into town.'

Samuel Boykin seemed to gain more poise. 'What kind of man are you, Allum? And the rest of you ... doesn't an order from your boss – be that a woman or not – mean anything to any of you? This is not what Miss Roberts wants, nor is it what Seaborn would've wanted.'

'Well,' said the big man silently. 'We are doin' this for both of them – Miss Mattie and Seaborn.'

One of the other riders chimed in petulantly. 'C'mon, Big Jim, we're wastin' time. Warlow has probably hightailed it out of town already.'

Over his broad shoulder, James 'Big Jim' Allum roared. 'Now just hold on, Leon!' He fixed a harsh look fully on Boykin and Asa again. 'Now, Sheriff, it's like this ... me and

48

the boys came into town to clear up some business that's been eating at us. Something that needed to be done for quite some time now. Believe you me, this town will be the better for it. Now why don't you and your boy deputy there get out of our way and let us take care of this.' He paused again. 'We can do this the easy way or the hard way, Sheriff. Choice is yours.'

Asa was silent, patiently waiting. Now, in Boykin, he saw the man's reluctance turn into indecisiveness. And worse, Big Jim noticed it too.

'Now that's a good boy, Sheriff. You just go find yourself a quiet spot and stay out of our way. What do you say, boys, about an hour or so?'

The other riders laughed.

Samuel Boykin shuffled to one side, eyes down, face bathed with a surly indignity. And right there, thought Asa Casady, was all the proof he needed that Boykin was not the man he had hoped he'd be. This was just a job for Boykin – room and board with a tin star to sport on his chest. There was no pride in the job or integrity.

Despite all of that, Boykin still represented the law – something Asa did too. Something these Roberts ranch hands had no right to dismiss. Asa's eyes began to smolder with anger and a heated purpose rose inside him.

Big Jim Allum was stirring his horse to movement again when Asa's voice hit him.

'Now hold on a minute, Big Jim!'

With those words, Asa moved out in front of Boykin, his voice taciturn and severe. 'The sheriff is not alone any longer. There are two of us. And this ends now!'

Big Jim pulled up rein again, staring back in utter shock. His voice was brisk. 'Who in the hell are you?'

'Casady is my name – Asa . . . Casady. But that's not important. What is . . . is this.' He pointed to the star pinned to his shirt. 'Deputy Sheriff of Alcove Springs. Why don't we just talk this out?'

The two men – Asa and Big Jim – were gaging each other. The strains of middle age had come and shown on Big Jim's temples. There was a worn look about his sun-torched face, product of a lifetime on the prairie. It wasn't a crazed, unreasonable face, Asa thought, but instead a face that was full of grit and respect. This was a good man.

Somehow, too, there was a hidden quality. His eyes furrowed at the corners in a way that suggested firmness, but also the character of an understanding and kind man. Here, thought Asa, was a man he could come to like, despite the threat that lingered between them.

'For God's sake,' rumbled Big Jim. 'You are still outnumbered, Deputy. You're new in town and may not be wise to how things operate here or what happened to our man – Seaborn Jones.'

Asa nodded. 'I am beginning to understand this town. And I know what happened with Mr Jones. And it doesn't change anything.'

The irked rider, Leon, spouted off again. 'Just another one of Akridge's men, Jim. Run him over!'

Asa's glance sought out the speaker, a thin, intense-looking ranch hand. 'Friend, I'm goin' to ask you to let Big Jim and I settle this matter. But make no mistake, I am not one of Akridge's men. Now, let's all decide to talk this thing out like civilized men.'

Big Jim Allum leaned forward in his saddle, crossed his arms on the saddle horn, and said, 'I like your spirit, boy. All right, I will listen to you . . . for a minute . . . no longer.'

Asa knew he had to choose his words carefully. 'Tell me the facts of the shootout between your man – Jones and Akridge's man – Warlow?'

'I know enough,' rumbled Allum.

'But not all the facts, right?' Asa probed.

'That fellow Warlow killed Seaborn – a good man – after he was caught bein' a cheat at cards. And if you aren't Akridge's man, why take this Warlow's side?'

'Ain't nobody takin' any sides,' Asa countered. 'All I'm sayin' is that so far none of you have any proof that this Warlow was actually cheating at cards. What the facts say is that this man of yours did accuse Warlow of cheating and supposedly went for his gun. And from the way Warlow and others describe it, Warlow shot your man in self-defense. All I'm sayin' is that we should find out the truth before rushing to judgement.'

The intense rider, Leon, suddenly dug the spurs into his horse. 'Enough talk! I'm done talkin', Deputy.'

He rushed past Big Jim, straight at Asa, who slid a quick step to the right, reached out and managed to grab the rider's gun belt and with a sudden tug, dragged the man out of the saddle. Leon fell, rolled on the ground, and came to one knee looking dazed and confused.

Asa, slightly crouched, was set to lash out at the rest of the riders, but Big Jim Allum got there first, his voice a mad growl.

'I got this, Jim!' Leon said. 'I will handle this tin star.'

The other riders, who had started moving forward in concentrated fury, slackened, and Big Jim shouted another command.

'Frank, get over there and take Leon's gun rig before he does somethin' really stupid. C'mon now, hurry on over there!'

The rider, Frank, was off his horse and ran over to the man, Leon, quickly. Leon stood now, his hands on his hips. He'd lost his hat and his hair nearly reached his shoulders. He seemed ready to come full at Asa, but Big Jim's growl clubbed him back.

'Now be patient, Leon, we don't know this fella or how he fights. He may not look like he's seen fightin', but a man can never be too careful. Bide your time.'

It had been a close thing, an abrupt eruption of violence that could turn deadly in a flash. Now it was over, that moment had passed. Asa nodded at Big Jim with a developing admiration.

'Thanks,' he said evenly. 'I have no beef with you. I . . . we . . . just want justice for Seaborn Jones.'

'Let us – the sheriff and I – do our job,' noted Asa.

Big Jim Allum waved his men to silence, his eyes intently on Asa. 'You a man of your word? I don't know you from Adam. You think you have the power to run one of Missouri Akridge's men out of town?'

'I aim to try,' admitted Asa.

Big Jim deliberated for a moment in stillness. Then he jolted his head in decision.

'All right then, partner. I'm a man who doesn't mind meeting another man halfway. But you listen now, we will be back in town. I want to see that you make good on your promise. And know this, if you and the sheriff cannot fulfill your promise, we will finish what we came here to do today.'

Big Jim reined his horse half-around. 'Back in your saddles, boys. We have wasted enough time today, let's get back to the spread and get our work done.'

The other men were reluctant to go. The fire in their bellies that had brought them to Alcove Springs was still ignited. But they were good men and they followed orders from Big Jim to the letter.

Asa watched the riders as they disappeared towards the slope to Roberts Ranch. He turned his attention back to the town.

Samuel Boykin was already about a hundred yards away, heading for his office. Down at the doors of Akridge's saloon, the well-dressed and keen figure of Cooper Warlow stood motionless – motionless until Asa's searching glance touched him. Then he slipped through the doors and out of sight. Over on the porch of the store Brinkley Blackwell, Mattie Roberts, and Carson Bird stood waiting. Asa went slowly over to them. It was Carson Bird who spoke first.

'We could see, but we couldn't hear much. I know Big Jim and that man is not one to scare off easily. What did you say to him?'

'I think I just promised to run Cooper Warlow out of town,' Asa said.

Brinkley Blackwell nearly shouted, 'You have put your foot squarely in the cow manure now.'

'I got them away from town, didn't I? That is what we all wanted, right?' Asa said brusquely. Then he added in a softer tone, 'I didn't know what else to do and didn't have a lot of time to think about it.'

He looked at Mattie Roberts. She was watching him, and now there was liberation in her hazel eyes. Her face and throat were softly sun-tanned, and the morning's sunshine did things to her skin, giving it a sort of radiance. Now that the stress of unease had left her, her mouth had relaxed into curves of a characteristic pleasantness.

Asa was happy to actually see the goodness in someone again; after word of his brother Alvin's death had reached him back home, he had become very morose. He gave her a smile.

'I admire Big Jim, Miss Roberts. I hope you won't go too hard on him or your other men, they seem like a good lot.'

'Big Jim is like the brother I never had. Thank you.'

Asa touched his hat and headed for the office, steadying himself mentally for the explosives he knew would be waiting there. For Samuel Boykin had been humbled and, after Big Jim's first severe statements, practically overlooked by all parties. So, unless the man was a complete loafer, he was bound to be in a brutal mental state.

No matter, Asa told himself, what had to be would be. A man could only play the part he was dealt.

Watching after Asa, Carson Bird cleared his throat and made an easy declaration. 'Does that man remind you of anyone?'

CHAPTER 5

Sheriff Samuel Boykin was sitting at his desk, bent forward, shoulders drooping, his eyes and face compact with a murky unfriendliness. Without looking at Asa Casady he rumbled, 'Might as well take it off!'

'Excuse me?' asked Asa.

'You heard me. The badge – take it off! You're done!'

Asa lowered himself into a chair and while he built and lit a cigarette, let the rinsing silence build. When he finally spoke, it was quietly. 'I think I'll leave it on. I'm far from done. I'm just getting started.'

Boykin smashed a hefty fist on the desk top. 'I'm the sheriff and I give the orders! I hired you and I am firing you!'

Their eyes met and were controlled. 'Really? I thought Akridge hired me.'

Boykin's look shifted, turned away. 'What were you thinking promising Big Jim that you would run Cooper Warlow out of town? Missouri will not allow that.'

'Is that so?'

'It is so.'

'In that case . . . guess you and I will have to do something to change Mr Akridge's mind,' Asa stated.

'You're a fool, boy!' Boykin almost shouted the words.

'No one can change Missouri's mind. Missouri Akridge runs this town. Make no mistake about that.'

Asa drew on his cigarette and let smoke out of his mouth. 'As I recall, Akridge wanted the boys from Roberts' spread headed off. I did that. That's a start.'

'Well, you also made a promise that you will not be able to keep.'

An icy starkness came out of Asa again. 'You are not understanding me, Sheriff. I stopped Big Jim, not because Akridge wanted it, but because they were not allowing the law to do their job. You should want that too.'

The sheriff grunted and folded his arms. 'You have a lot to learn, Asa, a lot to learn about the law, and, more importantly, the way of this town.'

In a surprise to both men, the door to the office opened and in walked Cooper Warlow.

'Gentlemen,' the man said. 'I've come to inform you that I will be leaving Alcove Springs for the time being.' He paused at the door as he had turned to leave. 'Good day.'

The sheriff leaned back in his chair and gasped. 'Well, I'll be damned.'

CHAPTER 6

Six months later

The man with the sky-blue eyes rode slowly across Bassett Canyon towards the Newport-Alcove Springs trail. He was flamboyant in watered silk vest, silken cravat and the type of stylish derby hat that was just then beginning to come into fashion in a lot of big cities back East. A few torn fragments of cloud floated across the Nebraska sky and their shadows moved swiftly across the summer brown earth and patterned the rooftops of distant Alcove Springs. The man's thoroughbred horse flung its head high then danced sideways as a Gila monster scurried across the faint trail, thick bodied and gleaming in the red dust.

He circled the town as he followed an Indian trail over the hard-packed earth and through drooping cottonwoods, riding easily until he reached the ridge country flanking the stage trail a mile north. He dismounted on a low mesa, ground-tied his horse, then walked towards the rim, taking a silver cigar case from the inside pocket of his coat.

The valley, the winding ribbon of trail and the town lay below him, basking in the brilliant sunshine. He smiled when he sighed, the distant plume of dust coming down the trail from the north. Horse and rider – even from this distance, he saw it was his one-time former ally, Emory

Dahlberg. He nodded his approval to himself as he watched the rider, as he touched a match to his cigar.

The finely dressed man – Cooper Warlow – was known as a gambler and, more recently, a killer.

Waiting for the man to come closer, Warlow heard the faint sound of singing coming from the town and turned his head towards it. On the sunny, Sunday morning air, it was possible to determine that the singing came from the little white church on the north side of town and he recognized the strains of 'Oh Lord, Let Me See Thy Glorious Face'.

Here, O my Lord, I see Thee face to face;
Here faith can touch and handle things unseen;
Here would I grasp with firmer hand Thy grace,
And all my weariness upon Thee lean.

Here would I feed upon the Bread of God;
Here drink with Thee the royal wine of heav'n;
Here would I lay aside each earthly load;
Here taste afresh the calm of sin forgiv'n.

I have no help but Thine; nor do I need
Another arm save Thine to lean upon;
It is enough, my Lord, enough indeed;
My strength is in Thy might, Thy might alone.
This is the hour of banquet and of song;
This is the heav'nly table spread for me;
Here let me feast, and, feasting, still prolong
The brief bright hour of fellowship with Thee.

Too soon we rise; the symbols disappear;
The feast, though not the love, is past and gone;
The bread and wine remove, but Thou art here,
Nearer than ever still our Shield and Sun.

Feast after feast thus comes and passes by,
Yet passing, points to the glad feast above,
Giving sweet foretastes of the festal joy,
The Lamb's great bridal-feast of bliss and love.

There was a big attendance at young Parson Maddox's church that morning. The floods had finally receded during the week, enabling the worshippers to travel in from the little spreads and some of the larger ones, encircling the town to give thanks for the bountiful rains that had broken the worst drought in memory. Hard, sun-dried men who hadn't been seen inside a church for years were there along with softer looking, better dressed citizens of the town, and they were giving the hymn all they had.

The Reverend Isaac Maddox, whose mission in Alcove Springs was no easier than it would have been in any other hard-drinking, sin-plagued town on the frontier, led the singing in his pleasant baritone and wondered if the unprecedented roll-up might mark a permanent improvement in the spiritual life of his town. He told himself privately that if any town could stand an improvement, it was Alcove Springs.

Over the tops of hymn books, ranchers nodded to friends they hadn't seen in months, and smiled. The atmosphere was just like that of a harvest-festival in Kansas, or a hoedown in Texas, when all the crops were in and everybody knew there would be money to pay the bills and maybe have a little left over for that new dress or saddle. The dams were filled, the creeks were running again and very soon there would be lush green grass. How could any man fail to be optimistic? Their smiling faces seemed to say they rocked the rafters.

The ranchers felt so good today that they didn't even resent the presence of the businessman in the front pew, even if he had been so tasteless as to show up at the Lord's house with his hulking bodyguards in tow.

A vastly rotund figure with a high, balding forehead and three smooth, round chins completely concealing his celluloid collar and string tie, Missouri Akridge didn't look like a man who might be the greatest threat to Alcove Springs since the Pedro de Villasur massacre, but that was his status with many a small rancher until the drought pushed everything else into the background.

Businessman, wheeler-dealer and self-styled empire builder, Akridge had won few friends during the spring and summer as he set about buying up the land of one small rancher after another in the immediate vicinity of town often at lower than market values, frequently, as rumor had it, with threats and coercion. The surviving cattlemen had seen something sinister in the dealer's octopus-like grab for all the marketable land he could get his hands on. But in the high spirits following the rains, and with the fat man present in church this morning, it was hard to work up much resentment, and more than one head nodded in his direction as Akridge turned to smirk cherubically at his fellow worshippers.

The unexpected attendance of Missouri Akridge, combining with the heavy roll-up, was the biggest lift the passionate young preacher had had in his few short months in Alcove Springs, and tended to offset his disappointment at the change in pretty Mattie Roberts, according to some of the townsfolk, since the new deputy, Asa Casady had come to town. From his pulpit, looking through the window over Mattie's golden hair, Maddox could see straight down the main street where Casady was patrolling near the bakery. Then Mattie looked up and smiled and he told himself that a man of the cloth had as much right to fight in the love stakes right up to the finish, and he waved his skinny arms energetically and led the faithful exuberantly into the next verse of the hymn.

Some distance away, the man with the shoulder length hair nodded in time to the singing until the sound was overcome by the slow beating of hoofs, and turning, he watched Emory Dahlberg cover the last slope to the rim.

The young Dahlberg bowed as he reined in. 'Long time since I last saw you,' he said.

'Anyone else know I'm back?'

'I didn't tell anyone.' He paused then asked, 'What have you been up to?'

'Business . . . my business,' Warlow replied, and tossing his cigar butt away, walked to his horse, swung up and led the way north.

The two men rode parallel to the stage trail for three miles, moving across the lower slopes of the Hogback Mountains. They crossed a bridge slung across a gorge and swung down into broken country.

They tied their horses in a thicket and Warlow removed his jacket and hat whilst the younger Dahlberg carefully removed the rifle he had carried across his saddle horn. It was a Winchester '76 repeater. Normally, Cooper Warlow worked with hand guns, but was similarly an expert with a rifle or shotgun. Holding the rifle in the crook of his arm, he nodded to Dahlberg, then started off along the ridge line in the direction of the trail.

Once Warlow stopped to rest, breathing in the clear, fragrant air. He felt a familiar excitement growing in him. He walked on with a small smirk and they soon reached the ledge where, hidden by rocks, they could stare directly down onto the trail. The stage road cut close to the ridge below, swung to the left through a narrow pass, then straightened up for the final run down valley to Alcove Springs.

Ferrill Dahlberg pointed noiselessly to the curve in the

trail at the base of the ridge. Warlow couldn't see the deep trench in the road which Dahlberg had carefully dug and covered with stick, canvas and earth. Warlow found it hard to imagine Dahlberg doing any manual labor, but secrecy was warranted this time. This gave him a little laugh. And if he couldn't detect it, then the stage crew would have no chance. He nodded in approval of Dahlberg's preparations, then settled himself comfortably, lying full length. He edged the Winchester against his shoulder and rested his cheek against the walnut stock and took an investigational sighting. That hymn was still running through his mind.

It was several minutes later when Dahlberg touched his shoulder and pointed north. Warlow saw the rising cloud of dust and jacked a shell into the chamber. The two men lay stationary between the boulders and the sun burnt stronger on their backs.

At last they heard the stage, the rattle of wheels, the crack of a whip and a shout from the driver. Then the lead pair swung into sight, the next pair, then the coach itself. The broad-shouldered driver was swinging his whip while the gun guard leant forward on the box seat, trying to see around the next bend.

The horses passed clear over the hidden trench but the stage joggled brutally as the front wheels dropped in. For a moment it seemed the vehicle would stand on its nose, but the rear wheels came down with an incredible crash and the coach jolted to a halt.

The gun guard was thrown headlong between the wheelers, but the driver somehow managed to keep a grip on the guard rail, though he had lost his hold on the reins. The near side door of the stage burst open under the impact, and a fat little drummer, cursing explicitly, was first to tumble out onto the trail, demanding complainingly what the hell was going on.

Nobody was quite sure as yet, and while they were still trying to figure it out, the remaining passengers, a middle-aged man and a lady, climbed down to inspect the damage.

This was the moment Cooper Warlow had been waiting for.

He eased his Winchester forward a little and grimaced as the sun glinted along the barrel. He fixed the sights on the stage door, then lowered them slowly to the gray-headed man's face. It was a face he knew well.

Warlow stared at the man's face over the sights. It was a handsome face, clean shaven and formidable with a stubborn chin. He lowered the sights to the man's shirtfront.

He stroked the trigger.

The rifle jarred; the coach vanished in gun smoke. Clearly through the crash of the Winchester, came a wild cry of horror. When the smoke cleared, the middle-aged man lay motionless on the trail with his son rushing towards him. The horses were rearing wildly and the gun guard was struggling up between them with his eyes darting wildly around. The Winchester spoke again and the woman screamed and was flung sideways. She clawed at the back wheel of the stage, threshing with a broken spine.

Warlow lifted the rifle and Dahlberg looked at him enquiringly. They had only contracted to kill the one man.

'That will serve as a reminder,' Warlow supplied, his voice as calm as though he were discussing what to have for lunch. 'That should be a bonus.'

Ferrill Dahlberg nodded reluctantly, and taking a last look down, they rose to leave.

They didn't hurry. It would take the stunned crew a time to cut the teamers free, then find the ambush spot, by which time the two of them would be long gone.

Warlow walked with a long and easy stride, feeling totally fulfilled in a way that not even his beloved poker could satisfy him. He was humming to himself as they mounted up and headed towards the mountains.

They had travelled some distance before Ferrill Dahlberg recognized the tune Warlow was humming. It was 'Oh Lord, Let Me See Thy Glorious Face.'

CHAPTER 7

At last the bright new brass sign was hanging just the way Asa Casady wanted it. He thrust the hammer into his belt and stepped back several paces to admire it. The sign read:

ASA CASADY
SHERIFF, ALCOVE SPRINGS

'Well, what do you say, Carson?' he asked with a wide smile. It was strange seeing his last name as Casady, but his time in Alcove Springs had helped him to forget about his purpose in coming to the town, to help heal some wounds, and to nearly put his past out to pasture. 'Think that will get any attention?'

Carson Bird, the well-made, brown-faced livery owner, chewed on a dead match and looked meaningfully up and down Main Street, Alcove Springs. The church service was still in progress and the Sunday morning main street was drowsily silent. Apart from a couple of depot hands waiting for the noon stage from Newport and three shirkers on the porch of Akridge's saloon, there was no one around.

'Well,' Bird drawled, 'I'd say that if any outlaws are comin' into town, then they'll certainly see where the sheriff is, Asa.'

Asa Casady – he was still getting used to that name – smirked. Carson had spent all Saturday and this morning helping him prepare his little office in time to surprise his former boss – the former sheriff and his new bride, due on the noon stage from Newport. A tough, young former ranch hand of the Roberts' ranch, Carson was deeply impressed by Asa's promotion to sheriff but doubted if he or any lawman could succeed in Alcove Springs. But being a good friend, he was too tactful to say so outright.

Just looking at that sign glinting in the sun reminded Asa of all he'd gone through to earn it. Many a time, it had seemed too great a challenge. He'd always had his mentor's support, but there was a limit to how far a struggling lawman could help in the town.

'Stage is late,' Carson observed as the town hall clock chimed the noon hour with no sign of the incoming stage.

'All to the good,' Asa replied quickly. 'It'll give us time to clean up before it rolls in.'

They'd finished tidying up around the office and were washing at the horse trough when the church doors opened and the congregation spilled out and flowed down Main Street. People stopped to admire the new sign, and more than one citizen came forward to shake Asa by the hand. Though Alcove Springs had been in existence more than twenty years, Asa Casady had only been in town for just over six months.

But there were a few in Alcove Springs who believed that the office of the sheriff was not a legitimate job with a man like Missouri Akridge in charge of the town. And he was one citizen who thought that Asa Casady's ascension could prove detrimental to the town's well-being, and had made no secret to the fact.

That citizen was rolling slowly by in a handsome rig with expensive cigar smoke trailing over one shoulder and a large pair of bodyguards seated behind him in his yellow-wheeled surrey.

Asa, who had just received a kiss for good luck from old Widow Blackwell, felt his smile tighten as he met Missouri Akridge's unblinking stare. He nodded distantly to Blind Willie McTell and Wade Lester, but taking a cue from their employer, Missouri's muscle men gave him the fish-eye in return as the vehicle rolled by.

The driver guided the carriage up to the tie-rack half a block along the street in front of the solid brick building that housed Akridge's saloon – The Missourian – and, upstairs, the living quarters and nerve-center of his business empire.

Missouri Akridge had come a long way in a short time in this area. But like most high-powered prosperous men, he had made many enemies – some intentional and some unintentional, and high on the list was Asa Casady. Even though Akridge controlled the town and its hiring process, Asa still managed to claim the sheriff's position.

Carson Bird watched Akridge in his carriage roll by. 'I swear he's gettin' fatter every time I see him. Looks like he's eatin' all them fine little spreads he's been takin' over.'

Asa understood his friend's resentment, for Akridge had gobbled up Bird's livery stable operation several months back. In fact, Akridge was trying to buy up all of the businesses, ranches and everything else in the area.

'Must be all the land and businesses he's eatin' up,' laughed Asa.

'Maybe we could have run that tub of lard out of town on a greasy rail,' Bird snapped.

'That's not likely, Carson.'

'Now, you're not aimin' to give me another lecture on law and order and doin' things accordin' to the book are you, man?'

'You sound like somebody who could use a sermon, Carson. Talking wild that way. You know what happens to those who speak out against Akridge?'

Carson spread his hands. 'Asa, look around. You're the new sheriff, and you're in a law abidin' town – far as I remember. God rest his soul, Brinkley would be ashamed of what this town is turning into. We've let a man like Akridge sashay in with a fistful of money and a lot of hard cases to stiffen his backbone, and inside a year, especially the last six months, he was able to trick, bluff, bully and thieve from half the ranchers in the area. I don't see any sign that people doin' things by the book, like you say, even slowed the fat man down. But I'm here to tell you that if he'd been run out of town on a greasy rail, or better still, horse-whipped out, Alcove Springs would be a better place right now.'

'Two wrongs don't make a right, Carson.'

'Seems to me I've heard you spill that one about a thousand times before.'

'You'll maybe hear it another thousand times too, Carson. I'll go on hammering those ideas until Nebraska comes out of the dark ages and realizes there are other ways of solving problems than the gun, the fist . . . or the greasy rail or the horse-whip for that matter. The law, Carson – the hope of the West and mankind's only effective weapon against anarchy.'

'Mattie has changed you, Asa,' Carson noted. 'Remember what brought you to town in the first place. But big words don't alter facts, and the simple fact of the matter is that your damn law never did work against the Akridge kind and never will. Would've thought you'd learned that by now – at least from Boykin.'

The argument grew animated, and it was an old and familiar one. Carson Bird was one of the founders of the town, and headstrong and inclined to violence. His idea of righting a wrong was to call out the person responsible, thump him on the nose, then have a beer with him after the dust had settled.

Asa knew the times were changing and those ways did not work anymore. Towns and states were turning more to the law to settle disputes. Asa had never – until arriving in Alcove Springs – believed in the law. Now he was fascinated with the law and truly believed that it would prove the salvation of the violent West. He'd lost many friends and a brother to the violence and was hoping not to lose any more.

His biggest task as he saw it, was to convince people like his good friend Carson Bird that he was right, and he set about attempting to do so now.

Then his new deputy – Dick Yancey – on his way to the stage depot, paused by the porch and remarked that the stage was now almost a half hour late.

That stopped the argument mid-fight, and both men showed concern as they stepped down into the street to join the deputy and stared north along the stage trail.

'You don't reckon something's wrong, do you, Sheriff?' Dick asked Asa.

A solid, firm man, Asa could only shake his head in reply.

'If you're thinkin' about a holdup, forget it, Asa. The stage isn't even carryin' freight today, it bein' Sunday and all,' Carson Bird noted.

'But there have been a few robberies in the past couple of months, haven't there, Sheriff?' asked Dick Yancey.

'That is true,' Asa admitted reluctantly, and was about to say more when they saw the cloud of dust rising behind the crest where the trail wound down from the mesas.

'You can quit worryin', men.' Carson smirked moments later as the coach loomed into sight. 'Here it comes.'

Jumping back onto the porch to collect his hat, Asa felt an overwhelming sense of relief, and at the same time was

69

angry at himself for letting himself worry that way. The truth was that he'd done a deal of worrying over the last few weeks before assuming the sheriff's position. For some reason he'd developed a presentiment of disaster concerning his brother's death over six months earlier and what had brought him to Alcove Springs.

Abruptly he stopped dead. Bird and Dick had moved out into the center of the street, looking unusually solemn as they stared up the trail. Somebody shouted from the stage depot. A man ran from The Missourian saloon, signaling.

Asa felt a chill go through him. He ran out into the street and stared at the stagecoach as it ground to a stop. Royce Dowden the driver was on his feet.

'Get the doc!' he bellowed.

Asa made a dash for the depot landing. The crowd was already congregating.

'Step back, all of you!' Raleigh Todd the freight agent shouted, and as the crowd parted, Asa saw the depot hands toting a body, too small to be his mentor, the former sheriff of Alcove Springs, Samuel Boykin, through the curtain of red dust. It was then he realized it was the body of a woman, who was unconscious but alive. Asa swung his eyes towards the gaping door of the stage.

'Sam?' he shouted.

Todd blocked the door, spreading his arms wide. 'Better not look in there, Asa,' he said, his face, full of concern 'Carson – you . . . Deputy . . . best get the sheriff away from here.'

'Get out of my way, Mr Todd!' Asa said in a voice he didn't recognize as his own.

'For God's sake, son. . . .' Raleigh Todd began. But he got no further as Asa seized him by the shoulders and thrust him away from the door.

'Oh no.'

The stage was filled with fine dust. A shrouded figure was on the seat. There was blood everywhere. Like a man in a nightmare, Asa reached out with a shaking hand, took the edge of the blanket in his fingers and whimpered like a man in pain even before he pulled it back.

The world spun – memories of the day he learned of Alvin's death flooded back to him. He had to grab the door-frame to stop from falling. He was staring down into Samuel Boykin's dead face.

CHAPTER 8

Asa waited until after the funeral. He waited until they had put his friend in the ground and after Doc Hansell had told him that his former boss's wife would be a cripple for the rest of her life. And only then, in the twilight of the following day, did he saddle up and ride into town to confront Missouri Akridge.

Carson and his wife Olla, who had been at his side always since the tragedy, attempted to deter him. So too did Mattie Roberts, the Reverend Isaac Maddox, the Roberts ranch hands with whom he had a run in on his first week in Alcove Springs. They all said the same thing: suspicion wasn't proof. Asa might believe Akridge had had a hand in the shooting of his brother, of Mattie's ranch hand Seaborn Jones, and now the murder of Samuel Boykin, and most of Alcove Springs most likely shared his suspicion. But there wasn't a lick of proof to connect the fat businessman with any of these tragedies, and nobody could see any point in confronting Akridge and accusing him of them – not even the sheriff.

Asa, however, was unyielding. He was in an inquisitive state of mind. He felt an odd detachment as though there were two Asas – and maybe there were – Asa Boyd, his real name and Asa Casady, the sheriff of Alcove Springs. He was a lawman, and no longer a hot-headed young fool who'd rode into town six months prior on a mission of revenge. He was not going to Akridge this time for revenge or to make wild charges simply because Samuel Boykin and Akridge had been at odds for some time. He simply meant to meet Akridge calmly, discuss what had happened the way a level-headed lawman should, then coolly scrutinize through the man's answers and decide if there was any reason to assume that he might have a case to answer.

So he told himself anyway. So he believed even when he was escorted into Akridge's presence and actually accepted the businessman's extended grip and his condolences.

'Blind Willie, a whiskey for the sheriff,' Akridge ordered as Asa sat down in a deep leather chair. The businessman went around the desk to resume his own seat, then leaned forward on his desk, making a tent of his round fingers. 'An awful thing, Asa, a truly awful thing.'

Asa nodded slowly, his eyes going around the room. It was his first visit to Akridge's inner sanctum in the back of The Missourian, which occupied the ground floor of the building on the corner of Alcove Springs' main street and Missouri Avenue. It was opulent with silken drapes, rich pile carpet, furnishings of dark leather and polished wood. It had been upgraded since Asa's last visit. There was the scent of money – and a faint aroma of cooking fat, cigars and whiskey. Akridge, he knew, was a big eater, smoker and drinker.

Wade Lester stood by the door now, a lean, wide-shouldered man with a razor-slash of a mouth and watchful grey eyes. Lester was the handy one with a pistol, big thin Blind Willie was the muscleman with one cloudy eye – thus his name Blind Willie. The latter certainly looked the man of a henchman. Blind Willie moved slowly but with a certain ponderous grace as he brought the drink across the room.

Then he joined Lester by the door.

Silence filled the room.

Asa tasted the drink, then stared into the glass. When he lifted his eyes to meet Akridge's benevolent gaze, he felt the first twitch in his stomach. What if this man, seated so close to him, had really been involved or worse, ordered the deaths of Seaborn Jones, Samuel Boykin and his brother?

He frowned. This was no time for emotion, he told himself. He had to concentrate on the facts. He was the sheriff now and Akridge – by all outwards appearances – was a respectable citizen; he had been attending church service with his henchmen while the attack was taking place on the stage out at Smokestack Pass. And most important of all, he, Asa Casady, was the man who respected the orderly process of the law, who despised emotionalism and violence which had claimed his brother Alvin.

He cleared his throat and said, 'Reckon you know why I'm here, Mr Akridge?'

'I have some thoughts on that,' came the smooth reply. 'But humor me, and tell me why you are.'

'I'm looking at the motive for Samuel Boykin's murder.'

'And you think that I can shed some light on that for you?'

'I'll be frank, Mr Akridge. You and your men here have been buying up one ranch after another, one business after another.'

'And this would lead me to want to murder Sam, how?'

'You and Sam used to get into disagreements mighty hard,' noted Asa.

'So did my little sister and I when we were children and she is alive and well back East in Baltimore.' Akridge eyed Asa steadily then opened a desk drawer and took out a blue plate on which was a big wedge of apple pie. He started scooping the pie into his mouth. A trickle of the pie juice

74

ran down his chin. He chomped his way right through the pie and dabbed his lips with a snow-white handkerchief. Then he smiled winningly and slapped the desk with the flat of his hand.

'By God, I knew there was a reason I wanted you as sheriff, Asa! I like your style! Of course, I could be angry at what you've said, but because of the way you said it, I'll answer you as best I can.'

The big businessman rose with surprising ease and moved around the room on his small, neatly booted feet, belly and chins jiggling. He paused to tap an elaborately framed picture on the wall. He looked very sober as he halted, feet apart, hands behind his back.

'I've met up with considerable opposition since coming to Nebraska,' he declared. 'This has been hurtful.' He paused, then gestured dramatically. 'There's nothing sinister in what I'm doing in this town, son. I make no secret that I want to buy up every ranch and/or business around here. I hope to achieve my goal very soon. I've gotten fat off my success, no denying that. It is my intention to incorporate all these smaller ranches into one big cattle-raising outfit, bring in the experts, then sit back and watch the profits roll in. I'm not doing all of this just for myself. If I prosper, so too does Alcove Springs. Believe me, if this town has an enemy, it's not me.'

Asa nodded slowly. 'I guess I can understand why you want the land. But there's one big question. How badly do you want it? How far would you go to get what you want? I've heard things since I've arrived in town—'

'That I've used a strong hand, intimidation to force men to sell me their ranches and business? All hogwash. I'm wealthy and successful, and my kind naturally attracts enemies and malicious gossip. I can tell you here and now that my dealings with every man in the area have been strictly ethical. And that, my friend, includes your friend Carson Bird and this mess with Samuel Boykin.'

Asa stared into the fat man's face for a time then got to his feet.

'I'm sorry to have taken so much of your time, Mr Akridge.'

'Not at all,' Akridge said. 'Anything for you, Sheriff. I'm a businessman and murder and mayhem are not good for business. I want this settled as quickly as you do.'

'Thank you.'

'Splendid! So now we've cleared the air, perhaps we can talk business.'

Asa looked stumped. 'Business?'

'Unhappily, the world must go on. And my investors back East are impatient to conclude the purchase of more property.'

'Like the Roberts spread?'

The businessman nodded.

'Miss Roberts has informed me she is not selling.'

Akridge stared at him.

'But . . . but I naturally assumed with her current financial situation as it is . . .' Akridge waved his hands. 'Surely she cannot continue to operate the spread any longer?'

'As far as I know, she can, Mr Akridge.'

Akridge's expression changed. He snapped, 'I'd like to get this matter settled, Sheriff. I can show you the bank's papers and how far in arrears the ranch is . . .'

'The matter is settled.'

Blind Willie McTell stirred. 'The boss made Miss Roberts a fair offer, Casady. She'd be loco to turn it down.'

'Yeah, loco,' Wade Lester confirmed, and smashed a fist into his palm.

Asa felt a chill of fear and tinge of anger. Still facing the businessman, he said, 'I will speak with Miss Roberts,

76

Akridge. I doubt she will sell. The sooner you accept that, the better for all.'

'I can make her a more than fair offer, Sheriff.'

'Didn't you hear what I just said?'

'Sure we did,' said Blind Willie. 'You just said as the lady wouldn't want to stand in the way of progress, and that she'd be happier to move into town with you. Ain't that right, Wade?'

'Sounds like a sweet deal for the sheriff,' Lester said. Then he laughed softly.

Asa swallowed. He turned and started for the door.

Blind Willie blocked his way.

Asa whirled to confront Akridge, who studied him with the impassivity of a brass spittoon.

'I don't scare, Akridge!' he snapped.

'Why would I want to scare you, Sheriff?' Akridge asked calmly.

Asa lost control, the final barrier of restraint breaking down. 'You did have something to do with what happened. I see it in your face.'

'I suggest you calm down, Sheriff, you are grieving and not thinking properly.'

'Go to hell!'

'Blind Willie!'

Blind Willie McTell reached for him and Asa erupted into action with the violence he had professed to abhor.

He slammed his fist in Blind Willie's face. The henchman's nose was flattened under the impact. He crashed back into the door with a look of bovine surprise on his bloodied face.

Instantly, Wade Lester moved in, driving a vicious hook to the side of Asa's head as he made to close in on McTell. Asa twisted from the hips and drove his right fist into Lester's gut. The man bent over, his eyes bulging. His mouth gasped

77

for air but before Asa could follow up, Blind Willie let loose a roar like an angry bull and launched himself off the floor, arms flailing.

Back pedaling, Asa drove in a straight left that rattled Blind Willie's teeth. It was a good punch, but his last. A hard fist crashed against the side of his head, followed by a knee to the groin. Asa crashed against the desk and McTell swarmed over him, bringing big thumping blows down on his bowed head and shoulders.

He dimly heard Akridge yelling encouragement, saw Wade Lester's grimacing face coming towards him through a red mist. He struck out wildly but the blows continued to rain down. Now he could taste the carpet against his mouth. Jumping to his feet, Asa swung blindly and caught Lester a hard blow to the mouth. Next instant, Blind Willie McTell came in behind an overhand right that landed flush to the jaw. The world turned blood-red, then inky-black and he knew they were still hitting him as he spun into darkness that seemed to have no end.

CHAPTER 9

'What's the Englishman doin' now?' asked storekeeper Barney Hogan, peering through the morning mist at the Springview racetrack.

Casey Ripons, the blacksmith, growled, 'Still settin' in his coach smoking.'

The two had agreed to act as 'seconds' in a duel to the death between this Englishman who said his name was Billings, the foreign stranger, and Senator Lee Twitchell.

'I doubt the senator even comes!'

'Then what in the Sam Hill are we doin' out here?'

The blacksmith grunted. 'It appears we are wastin' our time. Let's go on home.'

The man in the coach, who passed himself off as an English gentleman, glanced up at the sound of their approach.

'Looks like the senator ain't comin', mister,' said Ripons.

'So we'll be gettin' on back home,' Hogan added in support.

'Relax, gentlemen, the senator is a man of his word,' said the man, in a passable English accent. 'He will be here.'

The two exchanged glances. 'Now, look here, Mr Billings,' said the storekeeper, 'we've been here best part of an hour and he has yet to show.'

'Billings' stared at him in cool silence for a moment. He

had steel blue eyes, dark hair and a thin mustache. Then he said, 'A man like your senator cannot afford to ignore my challenge.' His tone was pleasant but touched with steel. 'He insulted me by inferring I was a liar and will have to answer my challenge or live the shame upon his honor until the day he dies.'

The storekeeper started to say something then turned sharply at the sound of hoofbeats.

Some distance away, unseen among the trees, Ferrill Dahlberg waited.

'So, you see, the senator is indeed a man of his word,' the 'Englishman' drawled, as Senator Lee Twitchell rode into the racetrack enclosure and dismounted, 'as I expected him to be.'

Twitchell was dressed in a plain broadcloth suit and was carrying a case of pistols. Very tall and straight, with his face betraying the effects of a sleepless night, he approached his opponent, who, during the argument the previous evening had described him as 'a disgrace to the Senate'; he handed Barney Hogan the pistol case. Then he removed coat and hat, placing them neatly on the running rail.

'You all right, Senator?' the storekeeper asked.

'Never better,' replied the politician, whose fiery temper had often got him into trouble. 'Are you prepared, sir?'

The 'Englishman' got out of the coach and carelessly palmed the six-gun from the single holster he was wearing and passed it over to Hogan.

'Ready, Senator.'

Hands trembling, Hogan checked out the weapons then passed them on to Ripons. A breeze stirred the mist and for an instant the four men were obscured before the mist dispersed into tatters. The sun began to increase its ascension into the sky.

In a hoarse voice, Ripons gave his approval of the guns.

Reluctantly, the seconds loaded the pistols then passed each duelist his weapon. The 'Englishman', tall, sleek and wide shouldered, spun the chamber of his gun along his shirt-sleeve and smiled. Twitchell didn't even glance at his pistol. Ripons coughed nervously. Hogan took a scrap of paper from his pocket and from it read aloud the rules.

'You'll stand back to back and I'll start in counting. On each count you'll each take one pace until. . . .'

'I know the rules of a duel, man,' the senator barked. 'Let's get on with it!'

'As my gallant opponent says,' smiled the 'Englishman', 'get on with it.'

The two duelists stood back to back, each with his revolver slanted towards the sky.

'One. . . .'

The men began to pace away from each other in time with the nervous voice. 'Two . . . three . . . four. . . .' Through the waist-high tatters of mist they strode. 'Five . . . six . . . seven. . . .'

'Good God, Barney,' the blacksmith suddenly broke in. 'Stop this!'

'Eight . . . nine. . . .'

'Barney!'

'Ten!'

Twenty or so yards apart, the adversaries swung and faced each other. The burly senator and the tall, dark 'Englishman' both stood stiffly, their guns moving steadily out to arm's length.

For one brief moment they made a noble picture. Then both guns seemed to fire at the same time. There was an aching pause. Then Twitchell began falling back instantly.

'Senator!' yelled Hogan. 'You got to keep your distance for your second shot!'

But the senator would not fire again. For even as the

storekeeper shouted to him, Twitchell started falling. Like some proud old forest giant under the axe, he fell slowly and thudded face-down in the damp grass. The two townsmen ran to where the Senator lay and turned him over. There was a neat hole between his eyes, barely bleeding.

'We should've have stopped this!' Hogan lamented.

'We should've contacted the law before it got to this.'

'He was a good man.'

'Likely could have been governor.'

So they went on, mourning the man whose failing was his impetuous temper, a man already history. It took the stutter of galloping hoofbeats to bring them upright. The senator's aide, Ned Trapp, who had returned to Springview at dawn to hear news of the duel, stormed onto the racetrack, hauled his lathered mount to a halt and almost fell from the saddle. The two men stepped back from the body, looking guilty. Trapp stared at the dead figure in the grass, slowly dragging off his hat. He'd been with the senator nearly five years; kept him out of trouble all that time. But last night Trapp had been in Blue River preparing for the senator's visit scheduled for today.

Slowly he lifted his eyes to the two men.

'He's dead,' Trapp said. Like them, he found it hard to believe that hard-driving, vigorous Lee Twitchell was no more. Then, like a man moving in his sleep, he glanced about him.

'Where is . . . he?'

Ripons and Hogan stared around.

'He . . . he's gone,' Hogan exclaimed.

With a muttered curse, Trapp swung into the saddle and began searching. He found nothing but the set of wheel tracks that mingled with all the other tracks on the main trail. Reining in with impotent fury, he stared towards Springview, knowing the bitter taste of failure. Then he swung his horse and rode slowly back to the dueling ground. The first towners were beginning to arrive at the track.

'Who won?' a man shouted.

Trapp didn't know who had won. He was certain the Englishman's name was not Billings, and he was doubtful of the stranger being from England.

Trapp suspected that the stranger was a gun for hire and that the duel had been a carefully planned plot to assassinate Senator Twitchell within the framework of the European dueling code.

Ned Trapp did not know who had won the day. But he knew who had lost. The people of Nebraska.

CHAPTER 10

In the moonlight, the ugly bruises on Asa's face did not show as he saddled up in front of the Alcove Springs Hotel. Along at The Missourian, there was loud laughter and piano music, but out front of the hotel it was oppressively quiet now. They'd done their best, his friends and his brother, now they seemed unhappily resigned to the fate that he would go off on his crazy odyssey, perhaps never to be seen again.

Carson Bird stood at the top of the steps with tight white creases showing at the corners of his mouth. Carson was angry because he hadn't been able to talk his friend out of going on the hunt for his brother's and friend's killer. And Asa flatly refused to take Carson with him.

Mattie Roberts stood at his side, dabbing her eyes. Mattie had been a pillar of strength since the news of Samuel Boykin's death and sat up last night watching over Asa after Deputy Dick Yancey had discovered him lying unconscious beside Carson's old livery corral. Mattie wasn't concerned with the rights or wrongs of what Asa was doing, only in the fact that this young man she was growing to love could so easily get himself killed on his crusade.

The Reverend Isaac Maddox rested a consoling hand on the woman's shoulder. It was cold comfort for him to reflect that if Asa failed to return he, the parson, might stand a chance to win Mattie's attention. He shook off the thought. 'Vengeance is mine, sayeth the Lord,' he had reminded Asa. But Asa would not listen.

Now Asa was ready for the trail. He stood by his horse and looked back at the people who were so concerned about him. When he had lain in bed recovering from the brutal beating he had sustained at The Missourian, he had realized that there was little chance of proving Akridge's guilt by tackling the man head on as he had done. He had to find the killer first. That would have been his first impulse after the shooting, had he been in the state of mind that possessed him now. It had taken that beating to jolt him out of his shock and to reveal a stranger within himself he'd never known existed, a vengeful, ruthless second self, ready to tear up the rule book and take the law into his own hands.

The goodbyes were brief. He swung up into the saddle and turned away with a half salute and let his horse make his own pace along one of Alcove Springs's side streets. He said so long to the town. . .

His face twisted as he passed the little building that had once been the bakery. His shingle gleamed in the gloom of the porch overhang. It had taken him only six months to earn that rectangle of brass, and what good had it been to him in his hour of greatest trial? The austere god of law seemed to him to have feet of clay.

He stopped his horse at the freight landing of the Alcove Springs Stage and Freight Company. The buildings were deserted, with one light showing in the dusty window of the main office. There Asa sat saddle with his face in shadow and the moonlight shimmering on his shoulders, staring over the scene, so quiet now. He was remembering the horrified cries of the crowd when they jerked open the door of the stage and the look on his mother's grief-stricken face when news of his brother's death was told to her.

It was like a white hot knife turning inside him to recall it all, yet he remained there a long time, reliving the scenes in his mind. The pain of remembering weakened yet strengthened him at the same time. He hoped that in time the strength would override the pain until he'd become the kind of man he had to be to avenge the deaths of his friend and brother.

At last he heeled his horse on and, riding past the jailhouse, he saw Dick Yancey standing on the porch with a man in an old-fashioned sourdough jacket who was bigger than the burly lawman.

Asa touched the hat brim in respect, not to the deputy, but for his companion. James Allum was Mattie's foreman and the last hope of the small ranchers in the area, he felt. That was if they still meant to resist Akridge's takeovers. Though the most successful ranch in and around Alcove Springs, Roberts Ranch, and not directly affected by Akridge's land grab, the doughty Allum had supported Mattie and Asa all the way. Allum believed there was a place for Akridge and smaller ranchers and businessmen and women in the area to coexist. That put him at odds with Akridge, who plainly believed the smaller businesses and ranchers belonged where half of them were already, namely; someplace else living on their sale money or trying to start over.

Allum offered no argument when told of Asa's plans. Asa had sensed that the young sheriff understood that it was something he had to do.

So he rode from Alcove Springs by the light of the moon, a tall, young man with a battered face, pistol and rifle, a shattered world behind him and an unfamiliar world of danger and uncertainty stretching ahead. He left behind a new grave on Boothill, a girl with tears glistening on her cheeks, sad friends, happy enemies, and a brave brass shingle gleaming forlornly in a town where, it seemed, the law of the gun was still the only one that mattered.

It took him a month to reach the town of Springview, less than a hundred miles as the crow flies, from Alcove Springs. It was a month of lone miles, false trails, relentless gun practice, stubborn hope, and finally failure bordering on despair. He was green to the game of manhunting and revenge, though nowhere near as green as when he'd set out from home until his first arrival in Alcove Springs. Yet novice as he was, he already knew that his quarry was no ordinary man. Ordinary men, even the notorious kings of the owl hoot left some trace, some lingering scent.

The man who had slain his brother had come from nowhere and vanished into smoke.

Like the man who had killed Senator Lee Twitchell, or the man who had shot Sam Boykin from nowhere, or the man who had joined the posse who hunted down and killed his brother Alvin.

Deep in the mountains, Asa missed the first week's newspaper uproar over the senator's death, and when he finally heard about it, it made no impression. He was hunting a cold-blooded killer, not a duelist.

But two days ago, when exhaustion forced him to rest up near Smokestack Pas, he had heard more about the senator's death, which the law was now classifying as an assassination arranged by Twitchell's political enemies. A brief article on the matter in a Cheyenne newspaper had suggested that Twitchell's 'opponent' was in fact a hired gun, and one of great talent and ability to have handled that affair so capably, then vanishing without a trace.

After reading this article, Asa drew a map of the region and calculated dates. Twitchell had died three days after Boykin. A man could travel comfortably from Alcove Springs to Springview in three days. . .

He knew then that it was a long shot, knew it now as he rode slowly down Springview's main stem, searching for the jailhouse. But he was reduced to taking long chances. He owed Sam and Alvin that much.

Sheriff Hal Goodman was a wizened, stern little man who, unfortunately, had known Boykin and his brother well. He openly disapproved of Asa Boyd's mission, but was persuaded to discuss the Senator Twitchell killing readily enough. The killing, and the killer. . .

Nobody believed this gentleman Billings was a true Englishman any longer, for exhaustive investigation had failed to trace any man of that name in the country. As the lawman described him, he was a tall, youngish man with a slender, powerful build whose grace of movement was the thing people seemed to remember most clearly about him. There seemed some debate concerning his hair and beard coloring, but everybody who'd met the man agreed that his eyes were very blue.

That was all?

Almost all, Springview's lawman advised Asa. But because he was a friend of Samuel Boykin's, and because of the terrible circumstances that had brought him here, the sheriff of Springview took him a little further into his confidence. The Twitchell killing had ruined Sheriff Goodman, he admitted. The authorities had to find scapegoats and he was one. He was being replaced at the end of the month and was retiring to a chicken ranch near Butte. But though his days were numbered as a peace officer, Goodman had worked day and night on the senator's killing, and his labors had been directed towards checking every available record or snippet of information on every man in the northwest who'd been known to hire an assassin.

It had been a tedious task and Goodman couldn't say that

it had been crowned with success. For the only killer who came anywhere close to fitting the description of the notorious Billings was a notorious pistoleer who was reputed never to have worked outside his native California.

The name of that man was Cooper Warlow.

CHAPTER 11

The dealer's scoop gathered in Asa's chips and slid them away across the green felt. Long, educated fingers stacked them in neat piles, red on red, yellow on yellow. There was silence at the table except for the clicking of the bone chips. Under a green eyeshade, the croupier glanced up. He had a calculating, glittering eye.

'Want to buck the tiger again, mister?'

Asa deliberated. He'd already lost fifty dollars in this gambling hall in lawless Rio Rosa. Half his dwindling cash reserve. He fingered his chips for a moment, then nodded.

'Five dollars on six.'

The croupier nodded as he placed his chips on a square. Other bets were placed and the glittering wheel spun again.

Only half interested, despite the fact that he was losing, Asa studied his fellow players. Rio Rosa was a tough town, living up to its notorious reputation. It was known as a haven for gunfighters, a resting up place between gun jobs.

The group seated at the table were ordinary enough with the exception of the man they called Doc Hansell. According to his information, Hansell swelled his gambling earnings with an occasional gunslinging chore. Hansell looked the part, a tall, cold-eyed fellow with a pencil-thin moustache. He had been neither friendly nor unfriendly, but he'd said very little during the session and Asa decided it was time to try to change this.

'Last time I played the wheel was in Durango,' he offered.

Hansell looked at him. 'So?'

'At the Sundowner.'

'I've heard of the place.'

Time and money were running out. He took the plunge.

'My pard Warlow was in the game that night.'

Slowly the wheel clicked to a stop, the ball rolling into a slot. But no colors or numbers were called. All the men at the table, including the narrow-faced croupier, were staring at him. Asa Boyd – he'd gone back to his true name – was a young stranger in a town where the only heroes were bad men, where the common enemy was the law. He had just dropped a name that he already knew held a menace and mystery of its own, even amongst men like this. He was still a long way from sure that the man he hunted was indeed the infamous Warlow, yet with each piece of knowledge gained about the killer, his conviction was strengthening. Rio Rosa could well be described as the outlaw capital of the south-western Wyoming and Asa had put the place down as the most likely place a killer might stop off to rest up during a busy season with the gun.

In the heavy silence, Asa nonchalantly pushed back his hat and smirked sketchily. 'He lost.'

A fat man with an ugly knife scar running from brow to jawline looked at him increasingly. 'You say Warlow is a pard of yours, kid?'

'I did.'

'What'd you say your name was?'

'Yeah,' Doc Hansell asked softly. 'What?'

Asa sensed his long shot had missed. He'd hoped that by claiming association with Warlow, one of his associates might reveal himself to him. But it seemed he'd failed. The players only looked hostile, though of course there was a chance that if somebody did know Warlow he might reveal himself later. The seed had been sown.

'Boyd,' he supplied, getting to his feet. 'Asa Boyd.'

'You lose . . . Mr Boyd,' the dealer said in a funereal voice.

Asa glanced at the winning number. He shrugged and grinned again. 'Well, some days you've got it, other days you haven't. At least that was how old Warlow used to say, as I recall.'

Walking away, he was conscious of the eyes boring into his back. When he stopped at the bar to cash his remaining chips and looked in the mirror, he saw that all the players had returned their attention to the game with the exception of Hansell. In the mirror, he saw the man staring for a long moment, then he resumed his play.

Some of the tension ran out of Asa as he sipped at his whiskey. The game he was playing was a dangerous one. A stranger took a chance dropping big names in a place like this. Many a dark plot was hatched here in Rio Rosa and many a stranger rode into its crooked main street, never to be seen or heard from again. Just looking around about him now, Asa could see knife-scarred faces, desperate-looking men with guns, thin-lipped percentage girls, and the old, superior-looking standout like Doc Hansell. A pack of jackals and he was bracing them in their own lair.

He stared into the mirror and swiftly dropped his eyes. He'd become what he had to become, but it was proving costly. He'd just had a glimpse of a face that had changed years in a few weeks and he barely recognized the face as his own. . .

A flinty-eyed girl sidled up to him as he was deliberating whether to have another drink or head for his camp under the bridge. She'd been at the gaming table. He'd thought her about forty, but now realized she was still in her early twenties under the paint and the red gash for a mouth. Life had aged her prematurely, he thought. Like himself.

'Can I buy you a drink, ma'am?'

'I don't reckon you've got time for a drink, mister.'

'How's that?'

'What you said back there at the table . . . you'd best hustle on back to where you came from, mister. . . .'

'Why is that? Because I just happened to mention my pard Warlow?'

She looked at him steadily.

'That's just it. Warlow doesn't have any pards. Apart from his fat little rich friend, that hombre's world is just divided up into people he might shoot, and them he mightn't. No pards. Specially not young roosters like you what look like they should still be home with mommy. What are you tryin' to do? Get yourself killed?'

'You know Warlow?' Asa asked hurriedly.

The girl's face closed. 'He's been here.'

'Recently?'

'Reckon he could have been.'

'I was told he never worked east of the Rockies.'

'Told? Thought you said you knew him down south?'

'When was he here, ma'am?'

The girl looked around nervously. 'I didn't come here to answer questions, kid, just to tell you to mosey on.'

He took her by the arm. 'Hang on a minute. About this fat, little rich friend—'

'His sidekick or something, the only one he's ever had. Now—'

'And Warlow's eyes, ma'am? Are they blue?'

'Blue as the sky,' confirmed Rio Rosa's soiled dove. 'And the coldest damned eyes I ever saw in my life and I've seen some. Now that's it, kid. I'm takin' a risk even talkin' to somebody who could be law, so why don't you haul your freight out of here and get as far gone from Rio Rosa as you can while you can still ride.'

'Ma'am . . .' Asa began, but she was gone, threading her way through the tables, a slender figure in tasteless baubles with the smoke cloaking her like fog.

Asa surveyed the room and felt the hostility stronger than ever. He wanted to stay on, wanted to see if his words might bring any further result, but he sensed he might have played this hand far enough for one night. Besides, he was very tired now, and tired men could make mistakes.

He built a cigarette, adjusted the angle of his hat and went out into the night.

He realized somebody was following him before he'd travelled half a block. Two of them. He stopped twice and they stopped, and the second time he started off again, he glanced back to find that they had vanished. He walked on again.

It was dark in the long street with a gritty wind rattling window shutters and whipping paper down the walks. Thumbs hooked in his shell belt, he passed the Cowboy's Rest Hotel and headed on for the river and the bridge where he'd left his horse.

Fatigued though he was, he was still alert, and sensed rather than saw the stir of movement in an alley mouth ahead. Moments later he heard the soft scrape of leather on stone. He went for his gun as he threw himself to one side.

For a man who had always despised guns and gunmen, Asa Boyd's draw was impressive. Every day during the long weeks on the trails, he'd spent hours practising with his pistol. Always athletic, he'd quickly found he had a natural gift for the work. But this wasn't practice. This was the real thing, and as his shoulder hit the street, gun flame blossomed in the alley like some desert flower and a bullet droned past his face.

94

The crash of the ambush pistol was answered by the voice of Boyd's gun as it lost its own pale flourish of fire towards ghostly shapes in the darkness. A man coughed and cried out in agony. Boyd rolled aggressively as the alley was again lit by a hellish gun flare. A bullet slammed the earth where his body had been a split second before, then a white hot lance of fire went through his side.

He was shot.

The pain and the desperate consciousness that the next shot might be the last he would ever hear brought him springing to his feet, his gun propelling shots as he rose. The heavy head-splitting roar of his pistol shook the night, and by the gun glare he saw a tall figure twisting slowly, a dark hat plummeting, his Colt firing meaninglessly into the ground.

Then the man fell headlong and Asa's pistol hammer clicked on an empty chamber.

He didn't reload. He seemed frozen, whether by pain or the realization of what he'd done, he couldn't be certain. He only knew that he had killed for the first time.

Nobody appeared on the streets of Rio Rosa. Here the sound of shots in the night was not a signal to come running, rather a warning for the wise man to mind his own business.

A low moaning from the alley finally lurched him out of his trance. He started forward with pain biting into his lower ribs. Blood soaked his shirt and pants top. He tripped over one motionless figure and moved warily to the next. The man stirred as he knelt by his side and dimly made out the lean features of Doc Hansell.

The dying man's eyes glittered up at him with hatred. 'Dirty, lawdog son of a bitch. . . .'

'I'm not a lawman,' he lied, he'd taken a leave from his position.

'Bounty hunter then ... doesn't matter...' Then the gunman stirred. 'I figured you'd be easy ... how in the hell does a dude like you get to be so fast?'

'If I'm fast, it's because I've had to get that way. Somebody killed my brother and my friend, Doc. I've a hunch it was Warlow. I'm hunting him down.'

His words carried conviction. A terrible smile crossed Doc Hansell's face. The man was the fastest gun in town at the moment, and as such had offered to take care of the dude who talked 'educated', whom all at the saloon had mistaken for some kind of lawman. Doc Hansell and his sidekick had gone after the stranger with the lethal intention of ridding the town of a potential threat to them all ... only to discover that they were all wrong, that their 'lawman' was just another crazy man looking to square accounts.

Hansell started to say something, fell still and, with a jerky shudder, died.

Asa felt sick to the stomach as he strained to get to his feet. Two men dead and a bullet hit him. Leaning weakly against the fence, he rested a moment then stumbled on, one hand clutching his side. He reached the bridge. His horse whickered an acknowledgment. Feeling his senses leaving him, he scrambled onto his horse and kicked it into a run, following the course of the river. The wind blew cold now and the reflection of the yellow moon swam in the water. Somehow, he stayed on the horse's back until the lights of a solitary ranch house glowed ahead. With the last of his strength, he turned the horse's head towards the distant yellow square – and knew no more for two fever-ridden days.

CHAPTER 12

'Another slice of pie, Dick?'

'Have some mercy, Mattie. I've had two slices already. Try the Reverend. He burns up more fat sin-busting than I do all day.'

The third person seated at the table in the front room of the Roberts Ranch that Sunday afternoon, Reverend Isaac Maddox, held up both hands as Mattie Roberts turned to smile at him with knife poised over the pie.

'Gluttony is still one of the seven deadly sins, Mattie,' he laughed. 'And by the feel of my stomach, I've already sinned today.'

They all giggled then, easy amusement between good friends. It had seemed a natural thing for Mattie Roberts to have friends over after Sunday service when Asa Casady went away.

They sat around the table talking for some time before Maddox contended Mattie be visited regularly.

Acting Sheriff Dick Yancey was good company and, more importantly, he was not apparently interested in Mattie the way the reverend was.

They hadn't spoken of Asa today, but as Mattie took her place on the swing seat on the porch, Dick asked, 'Any word, Mattie?'

'None. You?'

'Nothing.'

'It'll be almost six months Saturday since he rode off alone.'

'Six months can be a long time, can't it?'

'In this man's country, it surely can. Anything new on Akridge since I was in town last?'

'I believe he's out of town. I saw Roy Powers from the Blue River Ranch Wednesday, and he said Akridge had been out to warn him against lending support to this Ranchers' Association. According to Roy, they had quite a heated argument.'

The woman grimaced. 'Dick, do you believe that Missouri Akridge does plan to merge all the area's ranchers into one giant spread, as he says?'

'I suppose not. Yet the strange thing is that if he has so much money to spend and is so anxious to boss a real cattle empire, he could have found better land. Nobody knows better than you that the valley land is the poorest around here.'

'Somebody asked Akridge about that once and he replied that he could make even a desert flourish. Your guess is as good as mine.'

'You haven't heard from Akridge since I saw you last?'

Dick shook his head. 'Matter of fact, the fat man hasn't broached the subject of selling since . . . the ambush. Maybe he's just being considerate, or maybe he reckons all you ranchers will fold easy enough if the other ranchers quit.'

She looked at him steadily.

'Do you ever wonder if Missouri Akridge had anything directly to do with Samuel Boykin's death?'

'Sure, I've thought about it. Something like that happens, you search anywhere and everywhere for a reason. Nobody can argue that Akridge stood to gain by having Boykin put out of the way.'

'I know. Three more ranchers and businessmen have sold out to Akridge since the shooting. They're scared.'

'We don't know who was behind the killing, Mattie,' Dick Yancey said quietly, watching the blades of the windmill turn sluggishly in the gentle breeze. 'I believe that the way it was done, there was never any chance from the start that we would catch the killer or discover his motive. I believe Asa was right in what he said from the beginning, that it was a professional execution.'

'I suppose that's true,' the woman said, looking distressed. 'But please don't say it, Dick.'

He looked at her understandingly.

'Think of Asa, to hell and gone somewhere on the trail of a professional killer, right?'

'Yes, Dick.'

'Well, you're not on your own in that. It keeps me awake nights too. He was good to me. But the thing I draw comfort from is knowing Asa like I think I do. Asa's one stubborn cuss. Look how he worked his way up to the position of sheriff. If he puts his mind to something, he just might run that killer down, and stay alive too.'

'Wasted months,' Mattie said gloomily.

The acting sheriff reached out and placed his hand over hers.

'Not wasted, Mattie. One day, Asa will have this out of his system and he'll come riding back and be patrolling the streets of Alcove Springs again.'

'If he lives,' Mattie murmured, and her eyes were bright with unshed tears when Isaac Maddox reappeared with coffee and a quip about saving souls being an easier vocation than doing the Sunday chores.

The three lapsed into easy conversation then and Mattie Roberts' strained look slowly disappeared. Isaac Maddox had become Mattie's escort since Asa had left the county, and a good friendship had sprung up between the parson, the acting sheriff and Mattie.

Through his friendship with Mattie and Dick and his interest in the affairs of his parish, Maddox had become increasingly involved with the quandary of the small ranchers who felt themselves threatened by men like Akridge and Dahlberg.

But in this, Maddox shared the attitudes of Mattie and Dick that legal and peaceful resistance to these men was the only way to handle the problem. Most of the dwindling Ranchers' Association members belonged to either one of two schools, those who were considering selling up and those few hotheads who supported running fat Akridge out of town on a rail.

The three didn't discuss these matters that afternoon. They were all young, and there was a limit to how long they could dwell on sober affairs when there was good company, fine weather, and an afternoon of ease stretching before them. They were discussing the upcoming church social, the strange case of the Widow Blackwell's pet goose whose mysterious disappearance had coincided with a great banquet amongst the lushes of Alcove Springs, the latest magazine story which they had all read in turn.

They were in good spirits and chuckling at one of Maddox's anecdotes about his odd bishop, when James Allum the foreman came around the corner to report a rider coming in from the hills.

'Thanks, James.' Mattie smiled. Then she said to the others, 'Likely one of my linemen coming back from a check of the line.'

They thought no more about it until minutes later when they heard the horse come through the yard gate. Turning their heads, they saw the horseman come around the wind-mill.

It wasn't one of her line riders. It was a lean stranger with deeply hollowed cheeks, bearded, grizzled-looking and dressed in patched denim and a battered remnant of a hat.

'Drifter looking for a job by his looks,' Dick began, but broke off at Mattie's sharp intake of breath. The woman's hand flew to her throat as she came up out of her chair.

'My dear Lord!' she breathed. 'It's Asa!'

Dick Yancey began to shake his head. It was not until Mattie was rushing down the steps and the horseman smiled wearily that he could recognize his former boss.

Asa looked like a traveler back from hell.

Asa touched the familiar butt of his pistol riding his hip. That meant something. It was its own kind of law, the law he'd always detested, the kind of law that got his brother killed, but which circumstances had forced him to embrace. The law of courts and judges would never bring the killer of his brother and Samuel Boykin down, but a bullet from his pistol just might.

It was his first visit to Alcove Springs since his return to the area and Mattie Roberts' ranch a week prior. A lot of rest and Mattie's cooking had packed some weight back onto his lean frame, but he was still gaunt. Twice at the lonely ranch west of Rio Rosa, the homesteaders had though he was as good as dead. He'd believed it himself once, but good nursing and an iron constitution had pulled him through.

The story he'd told on coming back was that he'd been jumped by road agents and shot. He hadn't told anybody he'd killed two men and never intended to. Doc Hansell and his nameless sidekick were already history, with no law to concern itself about their deaths, none to shed a tear at their violent passing.

Life was a hard business in Rio Rosa and it was the kind of life Asa Boyd – now again Casady – was rapidly adjusting to.

Opening the door, he paused for a moment, then stepped out onto the porch. The brass plate, set up with such high hopes, had begun to tarnish. He thought of the joy and pride which he'd expected the sight of that simple sign would bring to his brother's and Sam's faces, and it was like salt in a wound that refused to heal.

He stepped down into the deep dust and walked towards The Missourian saloon.

The noisy Sunday bustle ceased as the batwings bellied inwards and customers looked up to see his tall, gaunt figure outlined against the hot glare of the street. The silence held as he walked slowly to the bar and called for whiskey and people glanced nervously towards the green door at the rear which lead to Missouri Akridge's private quarters. There was no sign of Missouri Akridge, but Wade Lester lounged against the wall chewing a dead match and watching him increasingly.

He still didn't know, he thought as the sampled his whiskey and listened to the normal sounds slowly returning. He didn't know if Akridge or his business partner Emory Dahlberg had had anything to do with the shootings, wouldn't know until he'd run the guilty trigger man down.

The whiskey warmed him and he thought about Cooper Warlow. An unbeatable gun hand, so they said. Educated, clever, polished, a man with a taste for the theatrical, given to disguises. A professional gambler turned hired gun whom others feared. A killing machine. A gun only some wealthy men could hire.

This much he had learned during his travels, but doubted now that he could hope to pass as a client trying to hire a fast gun. There had been no public uproar over the gun battle in Rio Rosa, but the word would have gone out that a young man in dusty clothes but with the voice of a dude had gunned down two hard cases after a discussion about Cooper Warlow. They would be on the lookout for this man who seemed more than capable of doing his own killing.

Was Warlow his man?

Instinct and deduction strengthened the hunch that he was, mainly because of the ruthlessly efficient method employed to kill his brother. He'd learned that all killers had their style, and that none was known to be as ruthless and successful as Warlow.

He nodded to himself. He was as certain about Cooper Warlow as he could be about any man like that. Roy Powers, the homesteader whose place he stayed and recovered at told him of his brother's death. Powers recognized him as kin to Alvin and confided in him that he'd heard that Warlow was on the posse who tracked down Alvin. And it was believed that it was Warlow who'd delivered the fatal shot. Asa was already planning to cast his net for Warlow when he took to the trail again.

He hadn't told Dick or Carson or Mattie that he meant to resume his hunt as soon as he was restored to full health. They would only worry, and they could do that just as well when he was gone. He knew he had to stay on for a time, to build himself up, to help out around town. Dick was having a hard time of it as acting sheriff, while the Ranchers' Association had yielded further ground to Akridge since he'd left. Luckily there was a meeting tonight, and Asa meant to attend.

Somebody tapped his shoulder. A man he didn't know stood before him. He was short and blocky, with a mean mouth. His face had an unfinished look and ginger hair tufted out under his hat over big bat-like ears. He wore two guns thrust in the waistband of his trousers. Asa smelt trouble even before the man opened his catfish mouth.

'You're Boyd or Casady?'

'That's right. Who's asking?'

'Kean.'

'That supposed to mean something to me?'

'I work for Mr Akridge now.'

'Yes? I'd heard the fat man had hired more men.' Asa looked him up and down with thinly veiled contempt. 'What can I do for you, Kean?'

'Hear tell you're a troublemaker.'

'You have been misinformed. I was the sheriff for a time, but on a manhunt for the killer of the former sheriff. But I hate to disappoint a man. Are you lookin' for trouble, Kean?'

Kean's low brow rutted. He had a feeling Asa was laughing at him. 'I never go lookin' for trouble, mister, but I sure know how to handle it when I find it.'

'Like Cooper Warlow?'

Fielding Kean's eyes widened fractionally, then went blank again. But he'd shown enough to convince Asa that the name Warlow meant something. He wondered where Kean had come from, wondered where Akridge hired his henchmen.

He glanced down the room at Wade Lester. He had come to the valley many months ago with the reputation as a fast gun. A man like him might well know where Akridge could recruit specimens like Kean. Or superior gunslingers like Cooper Warlow.

He turned back to Kean. 'If you've somethin' on your mind, speak up. You're startin' to bore me.'

Color suffused Kean's flat cheeks. 'You've a big mouth! I figured you for that soon as you walked in.'

'And I figured you as a second-rater from the start,' Asa said with sudden vehemence. 'Now get the hell away from me before I prove you're third rate, you ginger-headed son of a bitch.'

The drinkers who had drawn closer to listen to the talk between Asa and Kean, blinked in surprise. Some of them had known Asa since his first arrival over a year before, yet they found him acting like a stranger now. A mean, dangerous stranger who sounded almost anxious to tangle with ugly Fielding Kean.

And in the forefront of these, unnoticed as yet by Asa, was Carson Bird. Carson had always been the more reserved of the two friends, and now he was playing the role of peacemaker once again as he thrust his blocky body between Asa and Kean.

'Hey! Just come to buy a drink, Asa,' he said with a forced grin. He glanced over his shoulder at the glowering Kean, then took Asa by the shoulder. 'But I reckon as how we might enjoy it more outside or over at your office, what do you think?'

'I think the company would be better, Carson, that's for sure.'

'You best be ready, Asa . . . is it still Casady or Boyd?' Kean mouthed, and brushed his palm over the walnut grips of his guns as Asa and Carson pushed through the batwings and went out.

Asa was conscious of Carson's curious glance as they proceeded along the street, but he ignored them. He was still excited by the brief brush with Kean. Such things had come to mean something to him. Once he'd taken satisfaction in debating fine points of law and order with an adversary. Now, he was ready to employ insult or violence to get a point across.

If he'd bothered to think about his change logically, he might have considered he was going backwards. But Asa now believed he was learning to win.

Beyond the town, he could see the Hogback Mountains, an uneven line against the sky, and the scent of the grasslands came to him on a breeze. The sun was low in the west, poised above the dark bulk of the mountains, splashing the steep slopes with orange and gold. It would be dark soon, he thought as they swung into his office. Soon it would be time for the meeting. He had a hunch it might prove a vital one.

CHAPTER 13

'And so, fellow ranchers,' Roy Powers wound up his address, 'let's decide right here tonight to stick together and make the Association work. The last time we met, every landowner present promised not to sell out to Akridge and/or Dahlberg, but since then three more have done just that. I suggest that the formation of a combine is our last chance. Me, I'm not strong enough to stand alone. Maybe none of us are. I hate like hell to see any one of us goin' down one by one. I don't want to see this area turned into one big spread bossed by rich men we'd never get to see, and I damn well know most of you feel the same. So do we agree to combine, or don't we?'

There was a big crash of approval and several hats flew into the air under the lights of the meeting hall. The small but involved crowd had listened in turn to each speaker discussing their situation and suggesting courses of action to follow. They had reacted positively, but it wasn't until Powers got up that they really came alive.

Standing by the wall, Mattie Roberts, Reverend Maddox,

and Asa were clapping their approval of Powers' speech when they realized that newcomers had joined the crowd near the doors. One was Blind Willie McTell, another a bouncer from The Missourian named Speed, and bat-eared Fielding Kean.

There had been talk that Akridge might try to break up the meeting. And it seemed the rumors had foundation as Blind Willie purposely shoved rancher Eli Jardine, then loudly accused the man of bumping him.

Asa wasted no time, moving fast, snaking through the crowd while Jardine was still searching for a reply to Blind Willie's aggression. The three Akridge men looked the worse for drink, and Speed was swearing at the unfortunate Jardine when a hard elbow slammed into the small of his back and almost knocked him over a row of seats.

'Hey, watch it, Speed,' Asa smirked as the three men spun. 'Who the hell do you think you're shoving?'

'Well, if it ain't big-mouth,' Fielding Kean said with relish, and lunged behind a cocked fist.

Asa didn't hesitate. With a fluent motion, he drew his pistol and slammed the barrel into Kean's face, splitting the brow from nose to hairline.

Kean hit the floor hard with crimson splashing from the malicious gash. A woman screamed and Roy Powers' voice boomed for order. But while Bob Speed recoiled from the hungry, enthusiastic expression he saw in Asa's face, Blind Willie slammed the pistol down with a lightning move, then swung a brutal kick at Asa's groin.

Asa side-stepped the kick, then drove the pistol barrel around in a long, looping arc that terminated under Blind Willie's ear. The giant's eyes glazed over. He started to fall, but not fast enough to suit Asa who struck again and the whole room heard the crunch of breaking teeth as the tempered steel caught the Akridge bruiser square in the mouth.

A sharp stutter of boot heels rose above the thud of McTell's falling body and Bob Speed was gone, pitching against the door in his haste to get out. Gun still in hand, Asa stared down at the prone figures, unaware that he was smiling, unaware of anything but the feeling of power, this visible proof that showed that his hard months on the trail had been a long way from wasted.

Blind Willie McTell was out cold, but Fielding Kean started moaning as he strained to a sitting position. His face was a mess with blood coursing down over his cheeks and running into the corners of his catfish mouth. Even so, he managed to spit out a vicious curse as he glared up through a red haze at the tall figure standing before him. His right hand kept moving, inching towards his gun belt, despite the fact that Asa now had his pistol trained directly on him.

Asa didn't warn the man to be still. He looked almost hopeful that Kean would make a suicidal play. It was the Reverend Maddox, coming in quickly with Mattie, Carson and Dick behind him, who called a warning to the man. Kean blinked up at Asa and his hand lifted from his side to his battered face.

Asa prodded his outstretched leg with his toe.

'Akridge put you up to this, didn't he?'

'Go to hell!'

The toe crashed into his ribs. 'Didn't he?'

'That'll do, Asa,' interposed Carson Bird. 'I reckon as how this has gone far enough.'

'What's the matter, Carson?' Asa dared him. 'Frightened we might put Akridge against us?'

'Don't tell me I'm frightened of anything, son.'

Carson Bird's voice was cool, but there was an unemotional rigidity in the old liveryman's brown eyes. Those eyes held Asa's with severe authority until he looked away, then Carson addressed the crowd.

'This is bad business, folks, and I guess you're all thinkin' that Missouri Akridge was behind it. Well, maybe he was, and if so that's another point against him. But even if he sent these fellas here tonight to mess things up, he and Dahlberg come off second best, thanks to Asa here. So I figure we let it lie and hope that if Akridge and Dahlberg and men like them did have a hand in this, they'll learn a lesson and realize we just won't be pushed around anymore.'

Heads nodded in agreement and men came forward to hoist the Akridge men to their feet. It was Asa who had done the damage, but everybody was looking for direction from Carson. Asa's performance had awestruck everybody, but there had been something threatening about it as well.

Carson said, 'Help them down to The Missourian, boys. And Preacher, I'd appreciate it if you went with them and explain to Akridge exactly what happened.'

'Be happy to, Carson,' Maddox replied. He turned to Mattie. 'You can go on over to the church and wait for me, if you so please.'

'I'll walk Mattie to the church,' Asa said. He smiled at the woman. 'That OK, Mattie?'

Mattie nodded her head. She returned his smile but it didn't reach her eyes. With a sense of shock, he realized that beautiful Mattie Roberts was not afraid of Blind Willie McTell or Missouri Akridge, or even what might happen to the people of the area in the uncertain days ahead. She looked as though she was scared of him.

Moonlight sparkled on the river.

'I don't want you to go again, Asa.'

'But I must, Mattie.'

'They could've killed you. They nearly did the last time. Won't you be satisfied until they succeed?'

'They? Who are they?'

110

'The outlaws and gunfighters and whatever other ruffians you have been mixing with, searching for what?'

'They're the ones who might lead me to him.'

'But you don't even know if this Warlow killed Boykin.'

'I think he killed my brother too,' Asa said quietly.

She looked at him. 'Your brother? Who? When?'

'My name is really Asa Boyd, my brother's name was Alvin Boyd and supposedly he robbed the bank here in Alcove Springs and was chased down by a posse, a posse consisting mostly of men like the two I fought tonight. Men hired by Akridge and Dahlberg. I believe Warlow shot and killed my brother.'

'And what if he did that? What will tracking him down bring to you?'

'Justice.'

'You want revenge, not justice. You want Warlow dead.'

Asa stirred, lifting himself onto one elbow and looking down into her face. He had insisted they take the longest way home by way of the bridge and the river. That look he'd seen in her eyes at the meeting hall had disturbed him, and he'd used every effort to put her at ease, then cajole her into better spirits. He leaned down and kissed her lips.

She returned his kiss with a passion that surprised him, that brought to mind memories of older, easier days when he was still new to town. He remembered men like Carson Bird and Brinkley Blackwell talking of a bright future, good days coming, things like the sanctity of the law and the fine future of Nebraska.

Listless days. Never to be seen again.

He rose, and taking her hand, drew her up from the sweet-smelling grass.

'Time we were getting back, Mattie ... before your ramrod of a foreman comes looking for me with a horse-whip.'

111

'Asa. . . .'

His fingers brushed her lips. 'No more talk tonight.'

She sighed, slipped her arm through his, then leaned against his shoulder as they started up the bank.

'You know, you've become a very strongminded man, Asa Boyd.'

'I've become what I had to be – especially dealing with a stubborn woman like you.'

They laughed effortlessly together and Asa wondered how long it was since he'd laughed as they started along the trail towards Main Street.

The first house they passed belonged to Wallace Clark. About a year ago, Clark had owned a double section in the area. One of the first 'hold-outs' after Akridge set up operations in Alcove Springs and began buying up land, Clark had sold out the day after a wheel came off his wagon on the old Indian trail and dumped him down a cliff with two broken legs.

Passing the pitch-black house, Asa remembered Sam's anger when he heard about the 'accident' and its aftermath. Samuel Boykin had gone to see Akridge directly, but the fat man's reaction to disparagement had even then been taking on a pattern. Politeness, innocence, and impression of sorrow that people could think evil of Missouri Akridge. He had gone through the same routine tonight, when the parson explained the happenings at the meeting, even though it seemed patently obvious that he must have instructed his men to disrupt things.

Asa Boyd had a feeling that Akridge would go on smiling benevolently and shrugging off every accusation until his businesses were dominant in the area and every small rancher or businessmen had either quit or was loitering around town, drinking up his sale money, like Wallace Clark. Unless he made a serious mistake. Or unless somebody . . .

maybe about Asa Boyd's size ... uncovered something against the man that might stand up in a court of law.

His jaw hardened at that. He could feel his teeth clench. A court of law! The phrase once sounded so simple and right, but hadn't entered his mind for some time. Maybe his transition from idealistic lawman to whatever he had become now was not as complete as he'd thought.

It was when he glanced back for a last look at the Clark house before rounding the corner that he saw a stir of movement in the shadows of the old cow barn directly across the street.

Call it a sixth sense, but whatever it was had been honed by his recent experience, quickened Asa's pulse.

'Down, Mattie!' he yelled, and with his left arm flung the woman violently to the street as his right hand raked at his pistol.

The shadow in the cow barn doorway became the menacing shape of a man with a gun. Asa dropped to the ground, away from the falling woman, belly-whopping in the dust. He snapped over onto one hip and his pistol came streaking up to firing level. He was a fraction too late. In the doorway of the old building, a finger pulled the trigger.

With a taciturn firm knot in his gut, Asa watched the muzzle spit fire. He imagined that he felt the heat of the explosion in his face. The bullet cut into the ground, into the dusty clay street where he'd sprawled an instant before. The ambusher was lining up for another shot.

Now there was deadly purpose in Asa's movements. In the background he heard Mattie's stifled cry of fear, from the central block came a shout of alarm. The pistol was heavy in his hand. He fired once, not taking time to aim judiciously, but hoping to put a bullet in the ambusher's belly. Nothing like a slug in the gut to break up a fight.

His first shot went a fraction high, chewing rotten wood

from the barn's doorframe. He triggered again instantly and didn't miss. The stooped figure twisted and fell forward. Mattie cried out in shock and Asa whirled his head towards her.

'Are you hurt, Mattie?'

'I'm fine, Asa, but. . . .'

'Stay put!' he broke in, and leaping to his feet, criss-crossed across the street and rushed through the weeds.

He held his pistol at the ready as he closed in on the cow barn. His lips were peeled back from his teeth. The still figure lay face down on the grass, outstretched hand still clutching the hot gun. The ramshackle old building was vacant. Stepping forward, Asa slipped his toe under the man's body and turned him over on his back. The face was bloated already, though the bullet had struck him in the chest.

It was red-headed Fielding Kean, and he was dead.

CHAPTER 14

The enquiry into the violent death of Fielding Kean took place in the Alcove Springs courthouse two days later.

The hearing attracted a big throng of people and there was a lot of talk about the possibility of Missouri Akridge and his partner, Emory Dahlberg, being indicted for incitement to murder.

Just about everybody was bandying those high-sounding words about on the morning of the hearing, but they had originally come from Asa Boyd.

Asa took on the role of 'acting' prosecutor, despite the fact he was not an attorney and was also the principal witness. In a swift, enthusiastic return to the interest of seeing the law and not a gun pass judgment, he'd sat up burning the midnight oil at his office trying to put together a case.

But Akridge had a real attorney – Howell Kimbrough – who was florid of speech and complexion, and the highest priced attorney in Lincoln. He proved he was worth his high fees by getting Akridge off, not only scot free, but with an apology from the presiding judge for any inconvenience he may have suffered.

Kimbrough was masterful. The defense based its case on the presumption that an employer was not responsible for an employee's actions outside of working hours, and elaborated by informing the court of Akridge's 'dismay and distress' when he learned that Fielding Kean had been provoked into making an attempt on Asa's life.

It was tough opposition for a young man with no law degree and Asa sensed early that he was fighting a losing battle. One by one, Kimbrough paraded witnesses who testified how Akridge had attempted to calm Kean, following the clash at the meeting hall and how in the end he'd seen to it that the hard case was given a drink and put to bed. But Kean had crept out later and apparently gone off to do his dastardly deed. Mr Akridge, speaking through his expensive mouthpiece, was duly relieved to find that Asa and Mattie had escaped the ambush unscathed.

So it went on, and the judge's finding and subsequent apology became mere formalities. There was a gathering of ranchers at the Reverend Maddox's church that night that was more like a wake, but Asa didn't attend. As the cattlemen sat at Maddox's long table, discussing the shooting and rehashing the likelihood of Akridge's involvement, Asa Boyd rode alone as he crossed the Hogback Mountains and headed south.

For a brief time, he'd let himself drift back into believing that the law just might be able to right grave wrongs. He'd been a fool. He was totally convinced now of Akridge's guilt, but men like Akridge and Dahlberg used the law as their own tool.

He didn't believe that any court in Nebraska could ever find Missouri Akridge guilty of even a misdemeanor while he was clever enough to hire others to do his dirty work, and could afford high-falutin' frauds like Kimbrough to tidy up the loose ends when or if something went wrong.

There was only one way to avenge his dead friend and brother and that was to find their murderer and kill him with a gun. A dead man couldn't dodge a noose or hire an expensive attorney. A dead man couldn't take refuge behind the law that Asa Boyd had once sought to enforce.

The trail led all the way into Colorado, then back into Nebraska and again into northern Colorado. His pattern was routine. Questions in saloons and trail camps on the high plains, drinking sessions with outlaws who might know Cooper Warlow, meetings with lawmen, some of whom treated him like a fool-hardy boy; and a few who took him seriously and tried to help him.

He traveled from Colorado to Medicine Bow, Wyoming, where he undertook a week's work as a mule-driver in a mining camp solely on the tip that one of the mule-handlers had once ridden the trails with Warlow. It was a bitter pill to swallow when, after working for a full week to gain the man's confidence, he got him drunk on paynight and discovered that the big secret of his past was that he'd run off from his ugly wife and ten kids back East. He'd never even heard of Cooper Warlow.

Asa left the mine with a week's pay in his pocket. Following a newspaper report of a murder that might have carried the Warlow stamp, he traveled by train to a small, no name town on the Platte where he found no trace of his man, but did meet up with Hatcher Vinson.

Vinson was an outlaw, a sawn-off, foul-tongued reprobate who had chain-gang scars on his ankles and at least ten bullet and knife scars scattered over his body. It was when he met Vinson by chance in a nameless dive on the riverfront one night that Asa decided to join the dark brotherhood of the outlaws. This, he convinced himself, could prove to be the way to meet his man.

Convincing Vinson that he was an outlaw wasn't easy, but due to his fraternization with thieves, knifers and road agents during his manhunt, he was able to drop all the right names and had a working knowledge of the jargon of the outlaw breed. Vinson liked his tough style which was now more real than sham and finally agreed to give him a try.

The outlaw bunch assembled at week's end and on the Monday, went off to rob the bank at Grattonburg. The job proved successful and bloodless and not being thrifty men, the robbers moved down to Clanton Junction on the Colorado border to rest up and blow the proceeds in riotous living.

Clanton Junction was an outlaw town where a man could raise plenty hell if he was young and had money to spend. In keeping with his outlaw image, Asa acted tough and reckless and Clanton Junction's hard-eyed girls seemed to like it. But though he brawled with the best and strode the streets with the gang, he was never drunk and he never stopped searching. He was looking for a tall, broad-shouldered man with blue eyes, but he was cautious about mentioning Warlow's name, no longer claimed friendship with the man as he had in Rio Rosa.

He was more cunning now. Experience had taught him that Warlow's name aroused strange reactions. None of the outlaws doubted his existence, indeed he was a hero figure to many. But apparently even amongst such as these, the man was more feared than admired, for Warlow had slain too many of his own murderous kind to engender any admiration amongst the hard cases.

Several days after coming to Clanton Junction, Asa heard that his man had been sighted further down the Platte River and he rode forty miles in a night to check it out. The rumor proved baseless and he returned to the Junction. He'd written to Mattie when he first arrived in the outlaw town and received a return letter the following Tuesday when the gang was preparing to travel south to investigate the possibilities of robbing another bank. The thought crossed his mind that he was now almost reliving what his brother, Alvin, had done over a year before. There was good news from home. The ranchers had formed their combine and there had been no sell-out since he'd left. They were holding their own, Mattie insisted, but reading between the lines, Asa could tell things weren't easy on her ranch. She naturally wanted to know when he would be back but Asa didn't touch on this in his return letter. His homecoming seemed further away than ever.

Missouri Akridge said, 'He refused six dollars an acre?'

'Key-rect, boss,' said Blind Willie McTell.

'It's more than his lousy dirt farm is worth on the open market.'

'I told him that, boss. But Todd said as the combine wouldn't let him sell, even at ten dollars an acre.'

'The combine. I'm up to my neck with that outfit.'

'Reckon as how we all are, Mr Akridge,' drawled Wade Lester. 'But of course, everybody knows that the outfit would fall apart only for Mattie Roberts. . . .'

The gunman's voice trailed off. Akridge put a sharp stare on him.

'Are you tryin' to tell me something, Lester?'

'I wouldn't try to tell you your business, Mr Akridge.'

'Then just make sure you don't start.'

'Of course, boss.'

There was no sarcasm in Lester's tone. He valued his employer, even feared him a little, for this fat little man was awfully treacherous, and worse – rich.

Blind Willie McTell cleared his throat and said, 'Boss man, you've already bought up eleven of the fifteen outfits in the basin. Ain't that enough?'

'My friends want it all,' Akridge replied edgily. 'And they're paying me money to get it all for them.'

'Your directors you mean, Mr Akridge?' Lester asked.

'What if we don't get all the land, boss?' McTell said after a pause.

Akridge swallowed and reached for a glass of buttermilk.

'They won't drill. The geologist and the well experts say they must be free to tap the basin anywhere they please, otherwise it's not a profitable proposition.'

'And you'd stand to lose your investment in the company?' Lester hazarded.

'My investment, plus all the money I've expended since I came here.' Akridge mauled a slice of pork, chewed wildly. 'I loathe to lose money.'

'Too bad about Roberts getting to strut around the town like a big shot,' McTell remarked.

'Yeah, too bad,' Lester agreed, watching the fat man carefully now. 'Guess that Roberts woman is a natural leader. Pretty too.'

Silence, whilst Akridge stared at Wade Lester.

'How much?' he said suddenly.

Lester raised his brows. 'How's that again, boss?'

'The son of a bitch charged $500 before . . . how much would he charge to take care of Roberts?'

Lester stifled a smile. Before a lawman's bullet had trimmed off a small part of his left lung and most of his cold-blooded courage, Lester had been a gunfighter of note, viewed by experts as one of the best. He'd never realized his potential, but he had met many interesting people on his slow way up the gunfighter's ladder and the quick tumble down again. His familiarity with the big gun names had proven valuable to Lester and his various employers, and he sensed it was about to prove useful again.

'I'd hazard a guess it is closer to a grand now, boss . . . considering his reputation and demand has grown. . .'

'A thousand dollars to kill one hard-headed rancher!'

Akridge sneered.

'Could save money in the long run,' McTell opined. 'Those smalltime ranchers will go to water once Mattie Roberts is dead and Asa Casady is gone.'

Akridge stared out of the window. He was a man playing for high stakes and he wondered briefly whether he might be throwing good money after bad in a frantic bid to recoup. The morality of what he was considering didn't bother him at all, and despite the precautions Asa had set up for Mattie Roberts, he was quite certain the man they were discussing could take care of Roberts successfully, providing the money was right.

The fat man exhaled. He had the money, but hated spending it more than anything. Yet once the decision was made, it was irrevocable and he was prepared to outlay his $1,000, more if he had to, to wind this thing up.

He looked at Lester. 'Do you know where Warlow is now?'

'I do, boss. Ogallala.'

'Ogallala? Isn't he taking one hell of a risk?'

'Coop told me once that the best place to hide is right out in the open where nobody would dare of lookin' for you.'

'I suppose he's staying at the finest establishment?'

'But of course, Mr Akridge.'

'Fetch me pen and paper.'

CHAPTER 15

After checking out the bank job, the robbers decided security was too strong and headed north for Dover. A Wells Fargo shipment was Hatcher Vinson's objective. The outlaws calmly discussed how many men they would have to kill to pull off the job. Asa sweated. They'd not harmed anyone in the bank job, but the Wells Fargo robbery sounded like a shooting match already. Maybe he'd stuck with Vinson as long as he should. . .

They camped at the Pourde River that night, and Asa made up his mind to quit the bunch before dawn, when Haley Waters rode in. Waters was Vinson's cousin, and unbeknown to Asa, was to join the gang on this job. Waters had been resting up from a bullet wound in Ogallala, and it was quite by chance that he started telling Vinson about a gambling man there named White who'd cleaned him out of nearly $400. Listening absently at first, Asa came alive when Waters mentioned that Mr White was in the company of a little, well-to-do fat friend.

He started asking questions then and Waters revealed that White was tall and broad-shouldered with about the bluest eyes he'd ever seen.

Asa Boyd retired unnoticed at two in the morning. He reached Sterling at daybreak, and pausing only long enough to trade horses and wire a warning to Wells Fargo in Dover, he sped onwards to Ogallala to discover that the gambler, Mr

122

White and his friend, had checked out just the day before.

Mr White had left no forwarding address.

Cooper Warlow rode down out of the hills at midday and crossed by the stone section marker of the Roberts Ranch. The homestead was in sight across the flats with the glinting ribbon of the Little Blue River beyond.

Warlow rode easily, his free right hand resting on his hip, the elbow jutting away from his body. He smoked a cigar and there was an expression of contentment in his blue eyes. Cattle lowed, cowboys snaked across the prairie. There was a hum of activity in the air that would increase as the week wore on. It was time for the fall roundup in Nebraska and the ranches were hiring.

Warlow was looking for a job.

He let his horse dawdle as he angled towards the headquarters. His mount was a runty Texas cow pony he'd won several towns and months ago. A lariat was slung over the saddle horn, and a battered bedroll was buckled across the pony's lean rump. Warlow wore faded Levis, a battered old brown hat, a kerchief that had been crimson once, and a pistol in a holster that was worn and cracked with age and neglect.

He looked the typical cowpuncher, as at various times he had looked the typical bank teller, lumberjack, Mississippi gambler and numerous other roles, including that of a fine English gentleman. Ferrill Dahlberg was camped back in the Pleasant Hills, waiting.

Warlow was not sure if he'd be recognized. He hadn't been in the area for a long time and his appearance was much different now.

The gambler turned gunslinger smiled when he thought about his stay in Ogallala. During the past couple of months, more and more people had come to realize that he was real, and not a figment of somebody's wild imagination. The law was on the lookout for him all over, and he'd had a US Marshal as a regular poker playing companion at the Front Street Saloon in Ogallala. His disguise there had been that of a gambler – harkening back to his origins – but he knew that it had been his sheer bravado in exhibiting himself so flamboyantly that had guaranteed the success of his role.

Fording a hook in the Little Blue River and crossing the ridge, his objective lay within rifle shot. His lips curled upwards at that; a rifle shot. There couldn't be any easy drygulching on this one. Roberts was tough for a woman according to his recollection and his information, and wary as well. This job would require planning.

Two cowboys from the corrals saw him as he came over the hill. They could be some of the lot that had come to lynch him almost a year and a half ago for killing one of their riders. They came riding across to challenge him and one wore a Colt in a cut-down holster, gunslinger style.

'Who in the hell are you?' the round-faced gun-toter barked. 'Don't you know this here is private property?'

'Yeah,' chimed in the one with jug-ears. 'You lookin' for trouble?'

Cooper Warlow could make his blue eyes go as wide and as guileless as a week-old fawn when he wanted to. He did so now.

'Apologies, I never seen no sign sayin' this was private property, gents.' His voice was pure country, right down to the last twanging vowel.

'Who said there were signs?' said Gun-toter.

'Well, if you don't have no signs, how's a fella 'pose to know he's on private property?'

'This is Miss Roberts' outfit,' Jug-ears said. 'And Miss

124

Roberts sure as hell don't take kindly to saddle-bums wandering in about her spread uninvited.'

'Most especially now,' added the gun-toter.

This last remark wasn't wasted on Cooper Warlow, who had been carefully briefed during his midnight meeting with Wade Lester and Blind Willie McTell the night before. Yet his face didn't lose any of its disarming innocence and amiability.

'Well, again my apologies, gents, didn't mean to cause any fuss. You see, I'm busted without a dime. I've been lookin' for honest work ridin' the range. Folks told me I might find work out this way.'

Their belligerence began to fade and after several more minutes of exposure to the Warlow charm, they were half apologizing for bracing him so hard, and offered to take him in to see the foreman – James Allum. The round-faced gun-toting cowpoke's name was Con Mosby, and the one with the jug-ears was called Vinn Fargo. Warlow smiled happily and allowed as how he would be much obliged if they would do that. Warlow told him his name was Clem Brown, and they believed him.

On the way in, Mosby and Fargo told him about the tension on the Little Blue River these days. They didn't say it in so many words, but they implied that the situation on the spread stemmed from a fear for Roberts' life. Warlow clucked with concern, and laughed a big belly laugh inside. He'd show them soon enough just what sort of danger Miss Mattie Roberts was really in. That was a gold-plated certainty.

He saw more hands lounging around the headquarters doing nothing but looking tough when they reached the yard. They carried pistols and some had rifles, there were five of them.

'Ridin' shotgun on Miss Roberts,' Mosby supplied.

'You don't say,' Warlow responded.

The man standing on the house porch strode down the steps with a muscular swagger as they reined in. He started off a second session of cross-examination. He was James Allum, ranch foreman. Cooper Warlow gave him the same story he'd given the others. Allum was tougher to convince, but after several minutes he took his hand off his gun butt and decided that maybe Miss Roberts would talk to him.

While Allum went into the house, Warlow rolled and lit a cigarette, and chatting amiably with Mosby and Fargo, let his eyes run over both homestead and guards.

He'd expected to find the Roberts Ranch well defended. Since the formation of the ranchers' combine in the area, there had been a growing concern that Roberts, one of the instigators and leaders, might prove a tempting target for a person who had so viciously done away with the former sheriff, Samuel Boykin and forcibly made others sell and leave. The ranchers regarded Roberts as the lynch-pin of the combine and, more importantly, so too did the man who was paying Warlow's big fee. Warlow smiled as he remembered his previous time in Alcove Springs to the time he'd almost been lynched by the same men he was chatting with now. Akridge had vacillated about Roberts for a long time, afraid of public reaction should the rancher die the way Samuel Boykin or Seaborn Jones had. But Akridge wasn't so fussy any more. Warlow sensed that the man was getting pushed for time and money and had come to realize he could no longer afford to pussyfoot in and around Alcove Springs or he might miss out on the big bonanza.

From what he knew of that fat man, he'd drag the world down with him if he went to the wall.

The Roberts Ranch was big and prosperous-looking in contrast to most of the other area spreads, the killer noted.

There were neat, red-painted barns and sturdy fences. Apparently, Mattie Roberts was that rare breed, an idealist who could involve herself in other men's troubles even if she wasn't personally concerned. Warlow understood that the main reason for Roberts' involvement with the area ranchers was that she didn't want to see their land bundled up into one huge outfit, and that she had no time for Akridge both personally and professionally.

The hands around the yard looked tough, but to Warlow's expert eye, nothing special. Only one man stood out – a lean-bodied fellow of about thirty with bright red hair who leaned against the shady wall of the barn.

'Harry Lark,' Fargo said in answer to his query. 'New man, only signed him on two days back.'

A keener look came into Warlow's eye as he studied the lounging cowpoke from head to toe. He would have to be wary of newcomers or anyone who departed from the normal here. He was, as always, supremely confident of success, but it never paid to downgrade the opposition and he knew instinctively that Harry Lark was a dangerous man.

Mattie Roberts showed up. Warlow pulled off his battered hat with a smile. 'I'm mighty proud to make your acquaintance, Miss Roberts, ma'am.'

She raked him up and down with her sharp, dark eyes. When the silence continued, Warlow thought she recognized him – despite his appearance being much different than over a year before and the two never really meeting formally.

'Have you got an openin' for a good hand, ma'am?'

'I don't hire strangers.'

'So your boys told me.' Warlow twisted his hat in his hands and looked hang-dog. 'I'm sorry to hear as how you're kind of troubled here, Miss Roberts, but the truth is that I need a job real bad.'

'Yeah, you look kinda scratchy. What made you come here?'

'Well, mainly on account I heard so many good things about you the last place I worked.'

'Where was that?'

'Chet Shelline's Double S in Wyoming.'

'Chet Shelline's an old friend of my father's. You worked for Chet?'

'Sure, for the past three months. You can check on me if you've a mind, Miss Roberts.'

Mattie grinned. 'Well, that'd take time on account the Double S is over 300 miles from here and not on the mail routes, you know.'

Warlow knew that very well. With information supplied by Wade Lester, he'd concocted his background story very carefully.

'Matter of fact, Mr Shelline suggested I look you up when I came down this way, Miss Roberts,' he said.

Mattie pondered for a full minute. The spread needed more hands for the fall round-up, yet she must be careful about whom she hired. But this man sounded as genuine as could be, and running his eyes over his lean, wide-shouldered frame, she decided he looked like a top hand. And she could hardly deny that he looked as honest and as clean-cut as could be.

'What's your name?' she said at length.

'Clem Brown.'

The cattle rancher considered a moment longer, then turned to her foreman. 'James, find this man a bunk. He's hired at forty a month and found. He needn't start work until the mornin'.'

He was hired. He thanked Roberts, then let Mosby show him around. While they were in the bunkhouse, Warlow looked through the window and saw Mattie talking with the

128

red-headed Lark. They were glancing towards the bunkhouse and Lark was frowning. A hard one, he reiterated mentally before politely following his guide out to the cookshack.

Warlow filled in the remainder of the day familiarizing himself with the layout of the Roberts Ranch. There were about five hands, including himself, and a few of these, such as Harry Lark, were engaged full time in watching out for Roberts' safety.

'Comin' to somethin' when a fine, upstandin' woman like Miss Roberts got to go around her own acres under guard like a goldarned prisoner, Brown,' the gabby cook lamented over afternoon coffee.

'Just ain't right.'

'But if they'd butcher a fine man like Samuel Boykin, then there's nothin' they'd stop at.'

'Makes you wonder what the world's comin' to.'

'Of course, the boss lady could be safer than we think,' the cook went on. 'Samuel Boykin's former deputy and who followed him as sheriff has gone off hunting the killer again, and though there's them that say he don't have a prayer, I ain't so sure. Seen that feller when he was in Alcove Springs last week and he's sure mortal tough. Wouldn't surprise me none if he did catch up with that bastard sooner or later and then we could all breathe easy.'

'Reckon we can only hope and pray things turn out that way,' drawled Warlow, who had been brought up to date on everything the previous night, when he talked with Akridge's men.

The cook looked up to see Harry Lark walking slowly past with a rifle in the crook of his arm, and obviously drew assurance from the sight.

'Of course, we can look after ourselves here. The bastard'd find nothin' but hot lead and a cold grave if he ever come with hollerin' distance of this spread.'

'Certainly looks that way, cookie,' Warlow assured him. 'Certainly does.'

CHAPTER 16

'Warlow?' the man with the wall-eye said sluggishly. 'Is that name supposed to mean somethin' to me, mister?'

'I'm lookin' for him,' proclaimed the newest arrival in one-horse Mesa. 'My name's Boyd. Warlow killed my brother and my friend back in Alcove Springs.'

It grew very silent in Norton's Bar. The hairy Norton patted his heavy jaw and watched Boyd cautiously. A man encountered all sorts behind a bar like this, and often survival depended on sizing a man up from the start. But this grim-jawed young drifter whom the chill night wind had blown in, had him baffled. He didn't look like a fool, yet it seemed foolish for any stranger to enter a place like this and throw around a name like Warlow's without introduction. Norton was quite sure that if the legendary Warlow happened to be sharing of his hospitality tonight, such idiocy could prove deadly. As it was, some of his crooked customers, whose likenesses decorated law offices in other parts of the country, were already looking riled.

He said, 'Don't know nobody of that name, son. Why don't you try over in Dinnebito?'

'Yeah, why not?' snarled a thin man with yellow eyes, leaning at the far end of the bar. Kid Mohr was a gunfighter with lawmen dogging him from all over.

Asa glanced at the gunman uncaringly. Fighting and

131

trouble had become his way of life, but his heavy-handed manner here tonight wasn't designed to stir up a fuss, even if it may have seemed that way. He was tired, frustrated, prickly. He couldn't be bothered with ruses any longer. Now he came straight out with it. There hadn't been a whisper of a lead since he left home. He was beginning to wonder if all his obstinacy would produce anything but trouble of the kind that the man with the yellow eyes had in his face right now.

'I'm lookin' for a man named Cooper Warlow,' he said loudly to Mohr. 'You're not him.'

'Ride out!' the Kid replied. 'I smell lawdog on you!'

Asa looked at Norton. 'Give me a rye.'

Norton glanced anxiously along the bar. When Kid Mohr said something, he meant it. He was the fastest gunslinger in these parts.

'I said to give me a rye!' Asa snapped.

'You'll be dead before you drink it,' the gunman cautioned. 'If you don't haul your lawdog carcass outa here, pronto!'

The night wind wailed. It was cold outside and Boyd was so tired his bones ached. 'Come off the boil, mister,' he said, calmly enough. 'I'm not a lawman, at least the kind you think. I'll mosey along when I've had my drink.'

The Kid's pride had been tested. He moved away from the bar and spread his small feet wide apart. His right hand swung close to his gun butt and even wall-eyed Norton could see the death in his eyes. Boyd reckoned he could still avoid pointless gunplay if he ate crow and walked out, but suddenly he knew he wouldn't do it. He couldn't buckle under this kill-crazy breed, and in him there was another, darker reason for not walking away.

He turned his face to the gunfighter directly and lifted his tenacious jaw, a man so different from the boy who'd rode wide-eyed into Alcove Springs with the death of his brother on his mind and revenge in his heart.

'Draw on me and I'll kill you, mister,' he said.

That was all Kid Mohr had to hear, and with a soft intake of breath, he dipped his right shoulder and dropped for his gun.

The Kid was fast. He had to be, to survive in the world he'd lived in since his youth. But Asa Boyd, the man who'd polished a great, natural talent for speed and accuracy with endless hours of grueling gunwork over the long months, and who had already seen men fall dead beneath his pistol, was faster.

Boyd's pistol leaped and smoked and the exploding crash of the shot drove into Kid Mohr's slender body and spun him around. Mohr somehow caught his balance and was struggling to bring his gun up to bear when Boyd's six-gun spoke again. Mohr went down fighting, clutching dreadfully at the plank bar, then sliding down a barrel, leaving a red smear on the dark wood. A small booted foot stuttered briefly against the floorboards, then went still.

Boyd kept his cocked gun pointed at the white-faced drinkers as he slapped the plank bar with his left hand.

'I ordered a rye!'

Norton spilled at least two full shots in getting the glass filled. Boyd took it from his hand and then tossed the contents down his throat. Then he walked coolly from the bar without a glance at the crumpled figure in the corner, swung up onto his horse and vanished into the night.

The darkness drew its cloak about him as he let the big black horse take whatever trail it chose. Steel-shod hoofs rang on hard road. The lights of Mesa faded and died and there were no pursing horsemen in the night. Kid Mohr had lived the way he'd chosen and had died the same way. The Kid would think any man a fool for going after the man who'd beaten him fair and square. And nobody in Mesa wanted anything to do with a man who'd shown himself so much faster than their fastest gun.

Whiskey and nausea stirred in Asa's belly as the miles flowed beneath the horse's hoofs. But he didn't regret what had happened, rather the contrary.

He examined that thought, and the answer he came up with stirred a brief flicker of revulsion. For long weeks he'd lived with the possibility the day would come when he would face the man he hunted, man to man. And Warlow was said to be the fastest. Asa Boyd was fast too, but tonight in wind-blown Mesa, he'd had to find out just *how* fast.

Asa drew his hand across his face. Was this what he'd become. A gunslinger? He thought how his brother or Sam would be shocked – if they were alive – of who he'd become.

Mattie and Carson had shrunk from the violent hardness in him that they'd sensed on his last visit to Alcove Springs. He looked in his shaving glass each morning and saw a stranger with teak-hard skin and eyes like drills.

He saw a gunfighter.

Slowly he let his hand drop and the corners of his mouth lifted in a smile. He'd become a lot of things, he told himself, but there was no need for him to become a hypocrite as well.

He liked what he'd become.

He liked the sense of power; the way men looked at him now with shielded respect; the knowledge that he didn't have to rely on the law, a drunken judge or a fast-talking city lawyer to get justice.

He was now ex-lawman Asa Boyd – gunfighter.

The black horse pricked its ears at his sudden laughter, but the Colorado night wind quickly whisked the sound away.

Boyd's intoxicated mood, that both thrilled and disgusted

134

him, had spent itself by dawn and he found himself riding a featureless plain under leaden skies. A signpost indicated ARROWHEAD 5 MILES. He rode to Arrowhead where his sole objective was a hot meal, a bed and a day's sleep. Instead, whilst signing the register at the town's hotel, he overheard two locals discussing the strange client the storekeeper had had the previous afternoon. He had ridden into town on a horse that was big enough to carry his giant bulk, and he had spent five dollars on rice and soya bean sauce.

They didn't know his name, the locals told the gaunt-faced young stranger who suddenly started barking questions in an alarming way, but they were able to tell him that the man had taken the north trail out of town.

Within twenty minutes, Asa Boyd was riding an exchange saddler from Arrowhead at a flat gallop along the north trail. His heart thudded like a trip hammer as he used his spurs.

Just northeast of Arrowhead lay Alcove Springs.

By the time his first week was out, 'Clem Brown' was firmly entrenched at the Roberts Ranch. He rose early, worked hard and willingly, made himself agreeable to everybody and proved himself as good a cowhand as any of the others. One day he overheard the ramrod James Allum telling the cook he was a 'humdinger', a high compliment indeed.

The days on the spread, working cows, sweating honestly, and feeling the season drawing on, were highly enjoyable for the man some called the deadliest killer in the West. Warlow was a man of many parts – scholar, actor, thinker, gambler, cowhand, lover of the good things in life. When assuming a disguise he actually became what he was supposed to be and enjoyed every minute of it. But every role palled in time until he grew hungry for the only thing that ever made him feel alive – killing. And it was almost time to kill Mattie Roberts.

That Saturday night was paynight and most of the hands went into Alcove Springs. Warlow had planned that this would be the night, but at the last moment Roberts decided to go into town as well.

Philosophically, Warlow accepted that this would mean a brief delay in earning his cool thousand, but characteristically he made the most of the occasion. The spread was quiet by nine o'clock and the killer saddled up and rode off unnoticed into the Pleasant Hills to see Ferrill Dahlberg.

The fragrant scent of cooking beset his nostrils before he reached Dahlberg's hideout cave. It seemed that Dahlberg had ridden down to Arrowhead the previous day to stock up. Warlow reproved the man gently for in truth he'd become so absorbed with his range-work that he had completely forgotten Ferrill Dahlberg had only a few days' provision.

The partnership of the spoiled rich 'kid' Ferrill Dahlberg and the deadly killer was a strange one. A year ago, Ferrill had tracked Warlow down in California some time after Warlow had left Alcove Springs after a lynching party had been thwarted.

The two agreed to work together as hired killers, with Warlow as the gunman and Dahlberg as the business manager. It was an odd arrangement but one that was working.

Warlow returned to the Roberts Ranch before midnight. The ranch was asleep except for the nighthawks out watching the herd. Off-saddling and stalling his horse, Warlow stood in the shadows of the stables for several minutes, then on impulse, made for ramrod James Allum's room at the end of the bunkhouse. With extra hands on the Roberts Ranch payroll, things were crowded, and red-headed Harry Lark was sharing the ramrod's room.

Warlow reckoned he'd make further use of this quiet night and do a little checking on the one man on the spread who didn't seem to like the cut of his rig.

Allum and Lark had both gone to town with Roberts' bodyguard. The door was locked. Warlow picked it in fast time with a piece of fencing wire and let himself in. The faint glow of the stable lights was just enough to see by. He went directly to Lark's bunk and proceeded to go through his belongings in an open apple box nailed to the wall above the head of the bunk.

Shaving gear, writing material, toilet articles, tobacco, shells – in short, everything a cowboy might be expected to have. He went to work on the bed and was rewarded when a barely detectable lump in the bottom of the mattress turned out to be a wallet.

'That's more like it,' Warlow mused, and proceeded to examine the contents of the wallet.

There were three items in it: a photograph, an identification card, and a badge. The photograph was of Lark with notes showing height, weight and coloring. The identify card told anybody who might be interested that Harry Lark was a United States Marshal, while the badge confirmed it.

A vein began to thump in Warlow's temple. The crafty sons of bitches! They had hired a marshal to guard Roberts and had successfully kept it a secret even from Akridge. He was damned lucky he'd found out before making a play, for Federal Marshals were a dangerous breed.

He was about to replace the wallet when he heard a sound beyond the door. He froze. His hand fell to his gun butt, but he didn't draw it. It was too late for that. The door of the room was swinging inwards and the dim light sheened on a six-gun barrel. Harry Lark stepped into the room behind the gun with the foreman on his heels.

'So our hunch was right about you, Brown,' James Allum said, his face bathed with victory and fury. 'Who the hell are you?'

Warlow shrugged, hard-faced. He looked levelly at Lark and the lawman gave a small smile.

'You were just too right, Brown,' he said. 'You looked too much like the average cowhand. You were too good at the work. Turn around.'

Warlow turned slowly, hands upraised. Lark took his gun and shoved it under his belt. 'Make a light, James.'

Allum complied. Standing motionless, Warlow watched the man lift the lamp glass then feel for his matches. There would be a moment when the foreman turned up the wick when Allum was bound to be watching the flame. It would have to be then. He was unlikely to be given another chance.

Warlow didn't seem to move, but underneath his shirt, the sleek muscles were coiling, and rising in his blood was the excitement of imminent violence.

The match snapped into life in James Allum's hand. He applied it to the wick, and the room flooded with light. At that moment Warlow hurled himself backwards.

The killer felt his back strike the marshal's Colt barrel a split second before his driving elbow slammed into Lark's lean body with nauseating force.

Warlow spun violently and the Colt went off, the downward angling shot scoring the calf of his leg and the powder flash starting a small fire in the back of his shirt. The flying edge of Warlow's left hand caught Lark across the throat, but even as the man fell back, gasping for breath, he was trying to trigger.

Springing forward, Warlow snatched the concealed knife from his sleeve. So incredibly swift were his movements that he was able to draw the blade free and kick the gun upwards with his boot before Lark could fire. The shot sounded deafening loud in the room and the rafters shook at the impact.

Then Warlow struck, and with the instincts of a beast of prey, he went for the throat. It was an expert, savage blow

138

that laid Lark's throat open as though by sabre slash. The marshal's eyes bulged horrifically, a bubbling sound coming from his throat as he pitched lifeless back across the bunk.

Warlow threw himself to hands and knees even before turning his head. From the corner of his eye, he'd been conscious of James Allum's clumsy clawing at his hip while he dealt with the lawman, and knew even a hick ramrod couldn't take all day to come clear.

Two shots stormed, the first missing Warlow by two feet, the second by a whisker as the white-lipped foreman dropped his aim.

Pressing his hands against the floor, Warlow took the weight of his body and lashed out backwards with a double-footed kick that caught Allum in the shins. Allum gasped and stumbled. The killer came flipping upwards, turned in the air and struck with the knife, all in one dynamic burst of motion.

The dagger drove to the hilt in Allum's barrel chest. Warlow jerked it free and stepped back to give the ramrod room to fall. Then, picking up two pistols, he went out through the doorway in a great leap and hit the ground running.

He'd reached the stables before the first sleepy cowhand struggled from the bunkhouse, and before the first light went on in the big house. It was the works of seconds to throw a saddle on his horse, swing up and go spurring for the open doors.

A man was running across the yard with a rifle. 'Hey!' he shouted when the horseman burst into sight. 'Brown! What the hell is goin' on?'

Horse and rider looked twelve feet tall in the starlight. Warlow's lips skinned back in a wolf-like grin and the Colt in his hand burst into orange fire and the man staggered back with his hands clapped to his chest.

A shot from the bunkhouse licked the speeding rider as he went through the gateway at a gallop, but bending low over the animal, Warlow heard the slug whisper high. The next shot dropped behind but he was already out of range and storming across the plain as though the hounds of hell were at his heels, with the broken line of the Pleasant Hills set squarely between the horse's ears.

He had traveled a mile when, topping a hill, he brought the town trail into sight. Abruptly he leaned back on the reins, bringing the horse to a sliding, hoof-burning halt. Riders and a surrey. Roberts and the hands were on their way home from town. They must have heard the shooting, he guessed, for several dark shapes were well clear of the surrey now, riding for the headquarters with hands and heels flying.

Warlow instantly kicked his horse down the slope into a draw, and was angling off towards the hills again before the thought hit ... and a wild, exhilarating thought it was, at that. On quitting the headquarters, he'd intended to ride to the hideout, collect Ferrill Dahlberg, then make a dash for the back country. But the woman who was still worth $1,000 to him was close by, while her bodyguards looked as if they were all rushing in to see what the trouble was, when a professional would stick even closer to the woman they were being paid to protect.

Dare he try?

The very word 'dare' was like a magnet to a man who counted the milestones of life, not by years or dollar signs, but by the moments of high adventure when death yawned at his feet and only courage, daring and gun-speed could carry him through.

He pushed the horse up out of the draw and started north. As far as he could tell in the uncertain light, there were but three or four horsemen now traveling with the surrey, the rest were strung out along the homestead trail.

A soft laugh, and Warlow dropped out of sight.

A small stream traced the course of the draw. Crouched low, the killer rode through the water so as to raise no dust. Occasionally, he heard distant shouting from the headquarters over the sound of hoofs. He was close to the trail when the draw gave out. Rounding a gentle curve, he saw the surrey and four riders moving away from him less than 200 yards distant.

Lifting his Colt, he touched the horse with steel.

The stranger became aware of his approaching presence first. He spun in the saddle with a speed that impressed the racing killer, then brought his Colt to bear on Warlow with a speed that impressed him even more.Warlow fired, but the range was still too great for accuracy. Or so he thought. Next moment he was wheezing in pain as the slug from the tall young rider's gun scorched the inside of his knee and scored his horse's flank. The killer's smile disappeared. That stranger could really throw lead. Warlow fired again and knew he couldn't miss. But the instant he squeezed the trigger, the stranger's horse reared over backwards, throwing its rider violently then toppling down on top of him in a mad boil of dust.

Warlow lashed his mount to even greater speed as terror coursed through the remaining horsemen. Only Mattie Roberts kept her head, and was the only one to get her gun into play before Warlow opened up with both guns.

Cookie was the first to be hit, slumping across the splashboard of the plunging surrey with a mortal chest wound; but still trying to shoot back. Warlow's guns smoked twice more and two ranch hands plummeted from their saddles. A third ranch hand got off one wild shot before death claimed him with two thudding bullets in the head.

By now Warlow was abreast of the surrey. His horse leapt

over the dead horse and its pinned rider swerved to dodge another body. Cookie was grimacing at him with a death-white face and Warlow opened up again with both roaring barrels, not even seeing the small golden-headed figure on the leather seat before his driving bullets had flung her to the roadway.

Warlow swung about as the pinned rider shouted at him in a terrible voice. He only had to shoot, feeling oddly confused as his eyes were drawn back to the trailside. Then a man, wounded in the first ferocious volley, fired at him from up-trail and the close lick of hot lead jolted the killer out of his trance. He triggered at the lurching figure, missed. And he was the man who never missed. Frowning, he was forced to drag his horse sideways to dodge the next bullet, then spurred up the trail to throw off the man's aim as he brought his six-guns to bear again.

The guns licked against the heels of his hands and the cowhand lurched and shuddered like a Kiowa rainmaker. Warlow stared down at him as he raced past and felt no triumph, no tangy sense of thrill. The hoarse voice followed him and meant nothing. Something had happened to terrible Cooper Warlow and he didn't know what it was.

He let the horse slow to a lope when he'd crossed the Little Blue River. There wasn't a cattle outfit in the West that would have the guts to come after a man who had killed the way Warlow had killed.

He paused to light a cigar and examine the bullet burn on the inside of his knee. He dragged deep on his cigar then and headed into the Pleasant Hills at a slow lope, leaving the dying echo of violence in his dust.

CHAPTER 17

'A shocking business,' professed Gil Alland, chairman of Midwestern Oil, director of Akridge Enterprises, candidate for the Nebraska territorial legislature and, above all, prosperous businessman.

'Terrible,' agreed Ben Humphries, a feeble man in a classy store suit. 'All those people . . . including a US Marshal. Just awful!'

'I must say,' weighed in fellow director Clarence Dowden, looking disapprovingly at Akridge over the rims of his glasses, 'had I known things might go this far when we began, I would have withdrawn, regardless of the loss.'

Cleve Golden, the fifth man who completed the personnel of the determined Akridge Enterprises, considered Dowden's comments and eventually shook his balding head.

'Yes, I too,' he said in thickly-accented English, 'may have had second thoughts, had I known a little simple coercion could lead to such slaughter, Akridge.'

'Hogwash!'

All four stared at Missouri Akridge, who had delivered his gruff comment through a swollen mouthful of stew which had just been served hot to his office above The Missourian's barroom.

Assuming from Akridge's remark that he might not be in

total agreement with the sentiments uttered, concerning last week's bloody shootout on Mattie Roberts' spread, Alland lifted his sparse brows and said, 'We've yet to hear your comments, Missouri. Do you think you might stop eating long enough to give them?'

Akridge wasn't prepared to stop eating, but was certainly ready to express his genuine feelings.

'Crocodile tears,' he said vehemently. 'There isn't one of you who wouldn't fillet his own grandmother to get his hands on $1,000,000.'

The businessmen swapped glances as Akridge reached for the ketchup. There was no doubt about it, they were thinking, Missouri could be very blunt when he chose. But of course, they had known that when they first approached him to organize their venture into the oil business in the Alcove Springs area, and difficult though he may be, Akridge had proven himself the man for a very tough job.

The geologist's map on the wall by the windows showed him how difficult and potentially profitable the task of drilling for oil in the area really was. In the months since a shirt-tail rancher had detected a strange black seepage in his well, through the formation of the company and up to the present day, Akridge Enterprises had sought the expert advice of several different geologists, all of whom had been sworn to clandestineness. The geologists had proven unanimous that there were vast quantities of oil beneath the basin, and this in a decade where the word 'oil' was just beginning to steal the thunder of gold and silver. The geologists were also unanimous however, that due to the unusual geological formations in the basin caused by the Humboldt Fault, nobody could say for certain where a drilled hole would produce oil, though if a company drilled a series of holes in different areas, sooner or later they were bound to make a strike.

Therein lay the company's major problem, namely the necessity to acquire all the basin before commencing drilling operations, and to do so without revealing the true reason for acquiring the land.

The reasoning behind this was simple. Should the company merely acquire some of the basin and begin large-scale operations, within a week there would be derricks going up on all the land they didn't own, and it was quite possible that others would strike oil while they failed.

And the geologists and the experts spoke about subterranean reservoirs of 'black gold' that could net the driller countless millions of dollars. The minimum the investors expected to net from the great venture was $1,000,000, and there was something about $1,000,000 that could have a very calming effect even upon the most outraged conscience.

Akridge's plate was empty. He glanced hypothetically at the dish which the waitress had brought in, but decided against a second helping just now and wiped his lips with a napkin.

He looked like a caring Buddha as he leaned back in his chair and folded his soft hands over his swelling belly, but his words came out diamond hard.

'We might as well stop wailing about the Roberts Ranch massacre,' he stated. 'The furore's dying down and there are only a couple of posses still hunting for my man. It was an untidy business, I'll admit, but at least it was brought to a successful conclusion insofar as Roberts may have been eliminated by fear if nothing else.'

'You didn't know she had hired a US Marshal, Akridge?' asked Dowden.

'Of course not. But as it turned out, it was all to the good. The valley was stunned by the violence at her spread, but the fact that a federal lawman was also killed threw the fear of

God into her despite her not being taken out.'

'Some of the others too,' Gil Alland cut in. 'Are there any who are still refusing to sell?'

A grimace cut Akridge's brow, for this was the basis of his bad-tempered mood today. The fat man didn't give a damn about the Roberts Ranch massacre, nor the fact as a result he'd found himself being investigated by two federal lawmen to ensure that he had not been linked with the massacre. What troubled him was the fact that four ranches were still refusing to sell out.

The fat man explained and his partners looked astonished.

'But damn it all, man,' Humphries snorted in his phony English accent, 'when we were debating the removal of Roberts from the scene, you virtually assured us that by getting rid of her, the combine would fold and they would be glad to sell.'

'I know exactly what I said,' Akridge growled. 'I just didn't count on Alvin Boyd's brother, Asa, that's all.'

'Alvin Boyd?' asked Golden.

'You remember?' Akridge scoffed. 'He was our man we pinned the bank robbery on about a year or so ago. I am talking about his brother, Asa.' He shook his head ruefully. 'The damned irony of it. Warlow chopped down every man around Roberts that night or nearly, except Boyd, and the only reason he missed him was because his damned horse fell under him. If Warlow had known who he was, of course, he would have made a point of finishing him off. But he didn't, and now we've got the holdouts clinging to his shirt-tail.'

'Asa Boyd is still in town?' Clarence Dowden enquired.

Missouri Akridge's expression turned even more sour.

'Yes, he's still in town,' he finally replied.

'Does that mean he's no longer interested in chasing

Warlow?' asked Alland.

'Any news I get on Boyd I get secondhand,' Akridge clarified. 'But my boys tell me that after the Roberts incident, Boyd realized that he was the last hope of keeping the holdouts together, and decided that for the moment this was more important than tracking Warlow.'

'He almost did that, so I heard,' Golden said solemnly.

Akridge nodded. 'Very close. Apparently, he got a lead on Warlow's sidekick – Ferrill, followed him back to the valley. He came in to Alcove Springs that Saturday night and fired questions all over and soon learned that somebody who might have been Warlow was working on the Roberts Ranch. It was lucky for us that nobody took him too seriously. He tried to muster some riders to go out with Roberts' bunch, but they were too cowardly or apathetic. Had he got his men, they may have plugged Warlow.'

'I assume there's no chance of that killer being bagged, as you put it now, Akridge?' Humphries said.

'I hope not.'

'You don't sound sure,' Golden commented.

'He's still in the area,' Akridge said, and held up his hands as they all looked startled. 'Yes, I know it's a risk. But my man Lester tells me they have a perfectly safe hideout in the mountains, and Warlow is working on the assumption that with everybody expecting him to go as far and fast possible, the safest place just now is right here.'

'It sounds crazy to me,' Dowden ranted.

'I must admit it doesn't sound all that clever to me,' Akridge disclosed. 'But there's nothing we can do about it for, according to Lester, Warlow is acting strangely, taking little notice of him or anybody else.'

'Strange?' said Humphries. 'Was he injured in the gun fight?'

'A scratch and nothing more,' Akridge provided. 'But

enough of Warlow and the Roberts Ranch affair. The reason I summoned you to Alcove Springs today is to decide on our next move. What do we now in light of the fact that four ranchers, representing 3,000 acres, are still holding out?'

'Cut our losses,' said Cleve Golden. He jolted a thumb at the map. 'We already own two-thirds of the basin. Let us take the risk that we will see what the land we own will provide for us and commence drilling immediately.'

'No,' Alland said. 'I had an experience that has a bearing on this during my young days as a gold miner in California. Fifty of us were working claims in the Comstock region and just one man found worthwhile pay dirt. That mine, gentlemen, was the Comstock Lode which is still producing while the land around it is cattle graze. We just can't risk going this far and not going all the way.'

'I agree,' Dowden said. 'Missouri. . . ?'

'I do too,' Missouri Akridge held.

'Have you offered these ranchers more money?' Humphries asked.

'Double what the land is worth,' Akridge answered. 'They turned me down flat. And do you know why? It's because they are more afraid of Mattie Roberts and Asa Boyd than they are of me.'

'Then it's very damned simple as I see it,' said Alland. 'Boyd will have to go too.'

'Easier said than done,' Akridge bemoaned. 'I've never seen a man change so much in such a short time. He even traded lead with Warlow and lived to tell the tale. He's doubly tough and wary now.'

'I'm quite sure he is, Missouri,' said Alland. 'But I'm sure you'll agree that the problem of Asa Boyd merits further discussion?'

'Damned right I do,' Akridge responded. And they

discussed the Asa Boyd problem in their quiet business-men's voices while the chairman of Akridge Enterprises salvaged what was left of the stew.

CHAPTER 18

Asa came marching out of the heavy timber, leading a big stallion. For the best part of the morning, he had been riding and searching through the foothills. Now he topped a rocky ridge and paused, watching some trappers and traders.

Caringly, Asa stroked the stallion's neck. He felt like striking the blue-grey brute across its dreadful nose. However, he knew such a blow would have only stunned this mule but the big stallion merely blinked and stopped fidgeting. Boyd had bought the best horse he could afford after losing his last mount at Mattie's spread in anticipation of another long, testing hunt for Warlow. Due to conditions, his manhunting had been limited to scouting around the area, like today, but the blue-grey was still a fine horse, even if it had a foul disposition.

The trappers and traders worked in the sun, unaware of Boyd's presence. Boyd knew the men as he had checked with them three days ago. It was an easy ride down to check on them again, if he had the inclination, but at that time he did not.

He smiled gravely as he fashioned a cigarette. Likely the butcher was away in the next territory by this time. Or even over the divide and heading home to California.

Sucking smoke deep into his lungs, he felt enduring discomfort in his ribs. Doc Perry had told him he'd cracked two ribs when the horse fell on him, but fortunately none were broken. He had broken a finger in his left hand, and sprained his ankle. But all the injuries were diminishing now and at times he only wished the memories of that crimson minute would fade as swiftly.

The sky was turning gold. Sunset wasn't far away. Tossing the cigarette butt away, he turned and led the horse back into the trees.

He didn't mount until he'd cleared the timber a mile further on, and when he swung into the saddle, he scanned the country ahead for a minute before starting off. He was as cautious as a hound dog in snake country. Few people doubted any longer that both Samuel Boykin and Alvin Boyd had died because of their opposition to Akridge Enterprises. The area was in the grip of fear that was even more critical because Akridge seemed impenetrable. Only a handful of small ranchers had clung to their land and they had, for one reason or another – one of the last, Mattie, had decided to go back East to consider her future in Alcove Springs – turned to Boyd.

He accepted the leadership readily, smugly. But never for a moment did he forget the fate of the previous leaders.

They would find Asa Boyd hard to kill.

His hand brushed his pistol butt as he traveled up a long, grassy slope and there could be no denying the strange pleasure the contact gave him. His concept of himself and others had crystallized sharply in the past week and he now regarded himself as a gunfighter. The peace-loving former and briefly lawman had come full circle and the price was high, even though Carson Bird found his new, hard-driving nature hard to accept.

So the price of anything worthwhile never came cheap,

he told himself, yet at the same time knew a vague sense of regret.

Realizing he was daydreaming again, he reined in his thoughts and concentrated on the terrain as he rode homewards.

Sundown found him overlooking the basin. It lay like a giant relief map below him. Cattle country. Basin country divided up into pastures, each section fenced and clearly marked.

Who, apart from Akridge and his associates, really knew what lay ahead? It wasn't reasonable that the Akridge outfit should just let the spreads they had bought go to hell the way they had if they planned to turn the basin into the biggest and best ranch in Nebraska, he mused. He no longer believed that this was their purpose. The land must have other value, great value for men to go to such lengths to acquire it.

Heading for the trail, he reflected on events immediately after the Roberts Ranch disaster. The law had converged on the area in force. It had made a great deal of noise, mustered posses, conducted enquiries and investigations, had even instigated a full formal hearing under the jurisdiction of a judge. The result of all this was that the weeds were beginning to appear on the ranches of those forced to sell and on the graves of those who had been killed. Cooper Warlow was still roaming at large and possibly right now in the act of killing again, and Missouri Akridge was still very much a free man with his appetite unrestricted by cell bars, a noose, or a bullet in his fat gut.

So much for the law, he told himself, unaware that a man who had truly rejected his beliefs would not need to keep reiterating his disenchantment.

But if there might still be a little of the lawman left in Asa Boyd, it was no longer apparent to the man who waited for him on the porch of the old ranch house when he rode in just on nightfall. To Dick Yancey, this stern, hard-bitten young man with the bullet scars and big .45 was not so much a lawman as a grim stranger who had elected to work with him and look out for him.

'No luck?' Dick called as Asa stepped down at the hitchrail.

Asa shook his head as he came up the steps.

'I reckon he's gone.'

It was Blind Willie McTell's idea. McTell had never forgotten that Asa Boyd had broken his nose and utterly reduced his rank in the town and employer. A man of restricted intellect but proven courage, Blind Willie had obstinately refused to be impressed either by the change people saw in Asa Boyd, or the stories of his deadly proficiency with a gun.

To Blind Willie, Boyd was still a local upstart who'd caused far more problems than he should have been allowed, and it was when Akridge confided that he might have to seriously consider expending a large sum of money to rid himself of this new leader of the combine, that the bulky bodyguard decided it was time to reassert himself. He and Wade Lester, that was, for Lester had also suffered at Boyd's hands. Lester, as well, needed something to raise his stakes with Akridge.

Lester agreed that if they both wanted to rise with Akridge Enterprises once success was achieved and the black gold began to flow, then maybe they had better attempt to regain the ground they'd lost with Akridge over the testing weeks.

It was McTell's idea that they make their move at the Autumn Ball. The town would be packed out, there would be crowds, noise, confusion and jollity, Blind Willie declared . . . a perfect set-up in which to stage a quick killing.

Though still one of the finest shots in the territory, Lester wavered again when McTell insisted that he would be accountable for the actual gunwork, but when it became apparent that further resistance might only reveal that deep, destructive streak of cowardice which hatchet-faced Wade Lester had managed to effectively conceal from his ox-shouldered partner, he gave in.

McTell had discovered that the combine members meant to address the dancers to keep their problems in the public eye. Boyd was one of the four cattlemen left in the combine – as he was running Mattie Roberts' spread in her absence. The plan was to cut Boyd down from the roof of the store and they could be back in the stag line around the front doors before anybody was the wiser.

Unfortunately for the plotters, Boyd heard he would be called on to speak. The old Asa, who'd loved words and their power, would have celebrated in the opportunity to talk. But that Asa no longer existed, while the lean, hard-bitten young man who'd taken his place had come to believe his words and speeches a waste of time, and action was the only valuable remedy for the world's ills.

So it was as Carson Bird was talking, Boyd soundlessly spilled out of the ballroom to enjoy a smoke in the empty lot behind the buildings. Nobody else had noticed the stir of movement on the dark roof of the store next door, but alert as always, Boyd did. Inquisitive, he climbed the fence and went to investigate. Then Blind Willie saw him, recognized him, and cut loose.

Lester was rolling down the roof slope on the safe side even before Boyd fired back. Lester knew McTell had fired too hastily, knew that Blind Willie, so overtly tranquil and self-assured, had panicked to see their intended victim scaling a fence a hundred feet away in the half-light.

McTell made his second mistake when he rose to follow

Lester. Three pistols bullets thudded into his back. There was a great clatter as he fell and Boyd was racing around the rear of the store as Lester regained his balance and dashed for the street. Gun flame cut across the yard and Lester felt the lead bite into his thigh. He spun and fired twice. Boyd lurched.

There was some satisfaction for Lester in knowing that he was still as brilliant a shot as ever. But a gunfighter without true courage was no gunfighter at all, and what was left of Lester's sand, deserted him totally when he heard Boyd roar, 'It's Lester! Head him off!'

Wade Lester fled from the uproar, threw himself into the saddle of the first horse he came to, then dropped low over the animal's neck and used his spurs. With a harsh pull of the reins, he then swung the horse south and went speeding across the rangeland towards the outline of the Hogback Mountains.

CHAPTER 19

It was almost dawn when Asa fell into an agitated sleep, but his sleep was profound and dreamless some two hours later when the knocking on a door interrupted.

Asa grumbled and turned over in his bed, blinking at the strange wallpaper of the hotel room. Lethargically he remembered the ball, the shooting, the session with Doc Perry, the near-riot at The Missourian when an angry mob gathered.

He tested his left arm and found it stiff but not very tender. Lester's bullet had ripped his shoulder. He'd lost substantial blood, but speedy attention by the doctor had balanced the worst effects. He'd live.

He grew aware of the hum of voices from the street, and swinging his feet to the floor, he padded to the window and looked down.

A throng of men was gathered before the hotel and he saw immediately that they looked anxious and frantic. Then he saw Dick Yancey and Carson Bird and Reverend Maddox amongst then and each man was carrying a rifle.

What the hell was going on down there? And if there was trouble, why hadn't they told him?

It didn't take long to find out, once he hit the street.

Thirty minutes earlier, a gunfighter had shown up at The Missourian to announce that he had come to settle a difference with Asa Boyd. Instead of awakening him, Carson called upon the combine members and every man in Alcove Springs who still had some manhood left to follow him to the hotel and settle the matter themselves.

Boyd was deeply overwhelmed as he stared from one familiar face to another. He'd believed for a long time that the man in the street in Alcove Springs lacked bravery, which explained why they had required such leaders like Mattie Roberts, or Samuel Boykin, and now himself. But they were not gunmen, they were just everyday men. That took courage and it showed they thought highly of him to be prepared to take such risks.

But, of course, it wasn't necessary, he assured them quietly. This was exactly the sort of situation he was best qualified to handle himself.

'Asa, you don't understand,' Dick reasoned. 'The man at the saloon isn't any ordinary gunman. It's Cooper Warlow.'

'Warlow. . . ?' Asa seemed not to breathe as he replied.

'Rode in with Lester,' supplied Carson Bird. 'He's waitin' down there on the porch right now. It's up to us all to handle him.'

'No,' Asa said in a voice as hard as a nail. 'He's mine.'

'But Asa—'

'*Mine!*' Asa growled, and only then swung to face the wide street, to stare along its length and see the distant figures grouped on the porch of The Missourian saloon.

Arms swinging at his sides, he started to walk.

Warlow stood with Akridge, Lester and a collection of the fat man's employees on the porch. Warlow caused a huge gasp to rise from the watchers crowded behind the doors and windows as he stepped down into the street and faced the oncoming Boyd.

Warlow was glorious in a pale cream suit, bright red waist-coat, a broad-brimmed hat. His coat was drawn back and the sunshine flashed on the cartridge rims in his broad leather belt, on the handle of his famous gun.

Boyd lifted his chin. This was the man he'd hunted so long. And this was how he wanted him, conceited, commanding, at his murderous peak. This was the man who'd killed his brother.

With fifty feet separating them, Boyd stopped. Warlow looked very serious, in sharp contrast to the eager expectancy on the faces on the saloon porch. There were no words, just the long, slow assessment, a muted and waiting time. Then a dog barked on the edge of town.

It was like a sign.

Asa's hand dropped down and he knew he had never been so fast, so deadly certain. Hand, arm and heavy pistol seemed all of a piece, and the pistol was leaping upwards like a live thing in his hand, eager for its killing work, when he realized he was staring down the yawning muzzle of a waiting gun.

Warlow staggered, so stunning was his disbelief. Boyd executed the fastest draw thought possible, and he'd been beaten hands down.

A throttled sound came from his lips and he expected the collision of the killing bullets in his body any agonizing moment.

The bullets came, but there was no way he could understand why – no way his brain could explain how this happened.

Boyd's finger tightened on the trigger and in the split second after he fired, he saw Warlow's face white and emotionless, like a man already dead.

One shot.

Warlow fell deliberately, unfired gun falling from his

hand. The dust of Main Street received him lightly. He wasn't dead when Boyd reached his side, but death was close. Crimson stained the fancy vest and a thin trickle of red ran from the killer's faintly smiling mouth.

'That was for my brother,' Asa said. 'And for Sam.'

Warlow stared at him with those sky-blue eyes, but Asa couldn't be certain whether he saw him or not.

The killer coughed and a fresh red line of blood ran down his chin. His head rested on the earth as he looked up at the sky. He tried to smile to show his last rebelliousness of the death's head mistress with whom he dawdled for so long, but it wouldn't come.

He tried to laugh, but he only choked on blood.

'Asa!'

It was Mattie's voice.

Asa shook his head and blinked. Faces came back into focus. He saw Mattie kneeling before him, cupping his face with her hands, his friends behind her.

'Oh, Asa, you're all right, aren't you?'

'Yes, Mattie,' he said, taking her hand and rising. 'Never better.'

Unexpectedly his voice lost its authority as he saw somebody swinging a rope among the crowd and he heard Dick shout, 'They're goin' to lynch Akridge!'

Asa couldn't believe it, until he saw the faces surging around an ashen-faced Missouri Akridge and the dazed Wade Lester. They were familiar faces of men he'd known for nearly a year and a half now.

Asa was thrusting through them, roughly shouldering men aside to reach Akridge's side. On his way through he snatched the rope from the towner's hand, and an ugly roar went up as he waved it before Akridge's face.

'Give me one reason why I shouldn't let them use this

159

rope on you, Akridge?' he snarled.

'Please, Boyd,' the fat man gasped as he was jostled roughly. 'For pity's sake, don't let them do it. It wasn't I who brought Warlow in . . . it was Lester.'

'He paid Warlow $1,000 to kill Roberts . . . he set up your brother to take the fall for the bank heist that he used the money to start his company,' Lester blurted out.

The mob thundered again and Asa had to shoulder men back to retain his grip on Akridge.

'Why?' he shouted. 'Why did you go to such lengths for this land?'

It was Lester who spoke. 'Oil. They say there's enough oil under the basin to float Hogback Mountain.'

'Gimme that rope, Asa. I'll fix it around his fat neck myself,' a man shouted.

'No!'

Asa's voice rang out like a gunshot. He shoved the towns-man back, then threw the yellow rope over the heads of the mob into the street. And because he was Asa Boyd, his voice comforted their anger, his presence dominated them. He lifted his hand for silence, and through the crowd, saw Mattie Roberts watching him uncertainly, hope dawning in her face.

And then he said the words that she'd hardly dared hope for, the words that brought a shine to her eyes and started her pushing through the throng to reach his side.

'No,' Asa said once more. 'There'll be no lynching in this town today. The law will take care of this man and all his friends. Call the US Marshals! Akridge will be tried by judge and jury – in the solemn name of the law!'